MUST LOVE PETS

Friends Fur-ever

Saadia Faruqi

SCHOLASTIC INC.

ISBN 978-1-338-78342-1

10 9 8 7 6 5 4 3 2 1   22 23 24 25 26

Printed in the U.S.A.   40

First printing 2022

Book design by Yaffa Jaskoll

MUST LOVE PETS

Friends Fur-ever

For the real Imaan, and the real Sir Teddy

CHAPTER 1

I have good news and awesome news. The good news: It's the first morning of summer vacation. No more Selena Elementary. No more teachers or disgusting cafeteria lunch. Especially no more tests.

The awesome news: I'm going to get a dog.

Well, it's just a plan at this point, but it's going to happen, I just know it. My grandfather—Dada Jee— says making up your mind is the first step to getting things done. So, I've decided that I'll be absolutely, positively successful in convincing Mama to get me a dog.

She's going to say yes very soon, I'm sure. After all, how many times can a person say no to something before they get tired and say yes? Or before they forget and "yes" slips out of their mouth by mistake? So far, she's said no—nope, no way, nada, NO!—forty-two times in the last six months. Maybe she'll say yes on try number forty-three?

We'll just have to wait and see.

I stretch, then check the digital clock on my side table. It's almost nine o'clock. I better go down to breakfast if I want to get a head start on my summer vacation.

The delicious smells hit me even before I reach the bottom of the staircase. Mama is making parathas and scrambled eggs in the kitchen. My brother, Amir, sits at the kitchen island, eating like it's his last meal. His short black hair sticks out in all directions like he's recently been struck by lightning.

"Hello, sleepyhead!" Mama says, smiling. She's already dressed in her work clothes: a plain white blouse and black trousers. "Salaam!"

"Hello, sleepyhead!" Amir echoes, his mouth full of food.

"Ew," I tell him. "Close your mouth."

Amir is six years old, and very gross. He laughs and opens his mouth even more. "You're Imaan the sleepyhead!" he says, pointing a spoon at me.

I decide it's better to ignore him. He'll never stop bugging me if I pay him any attention.

I turn to Mama. There's flour and eggshells scattered all around her. "Need any help?"

She gives me a grateful smile. "Just with the cleaning up, please," she says.

I already know this. It's always my job to clean up once she's done cooking. I pick up the eggshells and throw them in the trash can. Mama finishes the last paratha and puts it with the rest on the island. "Can you get your grandfather from his room? I've got to get to work."

I don't really understand her hurry. Mama's an accountant, and she works from a little office in the back of our house. It isn't like she actually has to *go to work* like other people. Then I remember I want her in a good mood so she can finally say yes to a dog.

"Sure, you go work," I say, waving her out. "I'll get Dada Jee, and then I'll clean up once we're all done with breakfast."

"That's great, *jaan*!" She kisses the top of my head, then turns to Amir. "Stay out of trouble!"

Amir laughs again. "It's the first day of summer break!" he replies. "Of course I'm gonna get in trouble. Lots of trouble!"

Mama gives him a stern look. "Dada Jee may have other ideas."

Dada Jee is our dad's father. He used to live in Pakistan, but he moved to California to be with us after Baba died a few years ago. I was six years old, and Amir was one. He's been our babysitter ever since, especially during vacations.

Don't get me wrong, I love Dada Jee. But his idea of fun is talking to his lemon trees in the backyard or napping in his favorite armchair in front of the TV. And if you accidentally wake him up, he yells at you.

I'm ten years old now. I have my own summer plans. No grumpy grandfather or pesky brother included.

Mama looks at me, her arms crossed over her chest. "What are your plans for the summer, Imaan?"

How does she always know what I'm thinking? I'm so shocked, I almost blurt out, "Get a dog." But I gulp it down and grin nervously. "I . . . er . . . spending a lot of time with London, I guess."

"London's silly," Amir says.

I glare at him. "No, she's not. She's my best friend. You better not call her silly."

"She is," he insists. "She's always wearing strange clothes and pretending to be a know-it-all."

"That's a suit jacket, for your information. And she's supersmart," I inform him. London wants to be a businesswoman like her mom, and she's the best student in our fifth-grade class. Like, straight As all the way. And totally not silly.

"Hmph!" comes a grumpy voice from the door. "You girls better not be spending all day around me. You're too loud and giggly."

I turn to my grandfather. "I was just going to get you, Dada Jee!" I say. "Come have some breakfast."

Dada Jee shuffles up to the island and sits down next to Amir. He's got white hair and uses a cane because he hurt his leg in some war a hundred years ago. Well, okay, not a hundred years. More like fifty.

"You're late for work," he tells Mama, pointing his cane at her.

Mama pops a piece of paratha in her mouth, then wipes her hands with a kitchen towel. "Okay, I'm going. Be good, kiddos!"

She leaves before I can ask her about the dog. I run after her. "Mama, wait! I was wondering . . ."

She stops in the hallway and turns around. "Let me guess, is this about a pet again?" She sounds annoyed.

"Not just any pet. A dog!" I tell her, trying to keep the smile on my face. "Dogs are fun, and they make great friends. And they protect you from baddies. They're almost like people, really."

She sighs. "Listen, Imaan. A pet is a huge commitment. You know I don't have time to take care of another living thing. I'm already taking care of all of you, and working."

I hop from one foot to the other. She's going to say no again, I can already feel it. "I would take care of it, not you," I say, trying not to sound desperate.

"Not really. You're at school all day. And you can't drive. So, it would be up to me to take care of it, drive it to the vet, and everything else. I'm not doing it. Sorry."

"But . . ."

Mama's not finished yet. "Besides, Dada Jee would never agree."

She walks away quickly. I stand in the hallway, trying not to stomp my foot. Even though she never said the word *no*, that's what she means.

That's forty-three nos.

I need a better plan.

CHAPTER 2

"What's on the agenda for today?" Dada Jee asks after we've cleared breakfast away.

Well, I'm the one who cleans. Dada Jee just points his cane and tells me where I've missed crumbs. And Amir runs around and around the kitchen yelling, "I'm dizzy!"

"If you puke, you have to clean up the mess," I tell him angrily.

He laughs and starts saying, "Puke! Puke!" like it's the most fun word ever.

"Well?" Dada Jee asks again. "The children's museum is free today . . ."

I can't believe he's offering to take us out somewhere. I look at Amir and shudder. Imagine going to a museum and watching a hyper kid bump into exhibits. No thanks. "Maybe later," I say. "I'm going to meet London in the park this morning."

"Okay, good," Dada Jee replies. "Amir and I will watch some cartoons. We can go out in the afternoon."

He drags Amir to the living room, and I heave a sigh of relief. I can't wait to see London again.

I get dressed in jeans and a blue top that says SUMMER RULES. Then I head outside. Our street is long, but we live at the end of it on a cul-de-sac. Our house and London's sit right next to each other, with a small path in between that leads to the neighborhood park. It's got a metal fence and a code on the gate that only the neighbors know.

Okay, the code is 1234. Not exactly genius. But still, it's safer than other parks that are open to the public.

Plus, it's been our hangout since forever, first with our parents (or grandparent in my case) and then alone. Mama decided last year that we were old enough to go to the park by ourselves, as long as we stayed together. London's mom agreed. It's weird how both our moms make decisions together, just like London and me.

I make my way inside the park, trying not to grin like a fool. This is my happy place. Big shady trees line the boundary fence. There's a breeze blowing, and the leaves rustle like they're whispering, *Welcome back, Imaan.* I know it's silly, but I have a zillion memories in this park, more than any other place. Special memories of Baba pushing me on the swings, throwing me a ball, giving me a ride on his shoulders so I could touch the leaves on those trees. Silly, but precious.

A few little kids are playing on the playground, but otherwise the park is nearly empty. I march past the benches to the picnic tables at the back. There's a little patio area where you can have parties.

Or meet up with your BFF.

London is already sitting on top of a patio table, her legs crossed. "What took you so long?" she asks. She's not wearing a suit jacket today, just jeans and a T-shirt like me.

I'm still grinning as I climb up and sit next to her, also with legs crossed. "Oh, you know, the usual."

She grins back. "Still trying to convince your mom to get a dog?"

London knows me so well. It's because we spend all our time together. We always have, since our moms became friends when we were little. "She says it's too much of a commitment," I complain. "Like, she thinks I won't be able to take care of it and she'll end up doing all the work."

London nods. "Well, dogs *are* a lot of work. Not like cats."

London has an old cat named Boots. She's a tabby and very, very cranky. She hisses at anyone who comes near.

I groan. "I need a plan. I need to show my mom I can be responsible."

"I'll help you," London promises.

My shoulder leans against hers. I know she won't let me down. "Just like you help me with all my ideas, right?" I tease.

"Of course! That lemonade stand two years ago would never have happened without my marketing skills. And what about last year's big birthday bash for your mom? Who organized the mani-pedis and nineties hit music?!"

I nod. She's absolutely right. I'm the one with the big ideas, but she's the one who helps put them into action. "So, what should we do?" I ask.

London doesn't reply. She's waving to Mrs. Jarrett, who lives a few doors away from us.

"Hello, girls!" Mrs. Jarrett calls out, waving back. She's older than Mama, and she always wears a housecoat with flowers on it. Today, the flowers are bright purple with green stems. She's holding her dog, Sir Teddy, on a leash, but he's so big he just pulls her along like she weighs nothing.

I sigh loudly. Sir Teddy is ah-mazing. He's a golden retriever, with soft fur, floppy ears, and a twitchy nose. Right now, he's barking madly at a squirrel that's halfway up a big oak tree. The squirrel turns and chatters at him like it's talking back. It's brown, with perky ears and a small white streak on its head.

I watch them until they walk away to the other end of the park. I'd give my right arm to have a dog like Sir Teddy.

London nudges me. "Earth to Imaan!" she says. "I got the new *Animal Crossing* game. Wanna come play?"

Does she even have to ask? We climb off the table and walk back to her house together, making sure we close the park gate all the way. One time, someone left it open and a toddler ran out on the street. Thankfully, there weren't any cars in the cul-de-sac, but the toddler's mom couldn't stop crying.

I still remember that day. Dada Jee gave me a lecture about being careful, even though I had nothing to do with it. But now I always remember to close the gate tightly behind us.

Back on our street, there's a big truck, and men

are taking furniture out. "Is someone moving in?" I wonder out loud. The house next to London's has been empty for a whole year. We keep hoping a family with kids will move in.

"Yup," London says, pointing. I look in the direction of her finger. Standing on the sidewalk is a girl our age, with blonde hair tied in a short ponytail, and a shy smile. She's got a big camera hanging on her neck like one of those wedding professionals.

"Hello, I'm Olivia!" she says, walking slowly toward us. "We just moved here from Seattle."

I examine her smile and decide I like her. "Welcome to Orange County, California!" I tell her cheerfully. "Do you like video games about animals? We're going inside to play."

Olivia looks back at her house. "I think I'm supposed to stay out here."

"That's okay—we can play out here instead." I flop

down on the sidewalk. "I'm Imaan, by the way."

London runs inside to get her Nintendo. Olivia sits down next to me, holding her camera on her lap. "You've got a pretty name," she says shyly.

I shrug. I think it's okay. "Thanks. It means *faith* in Arabic." I look at her camera. "You like taking pictures?"

She nods and fiddles with the strap. "It's a Canon," she says, like that means something amazing. "A birthday gift from my parents last year."

I'm very impressed. I have zero clue what a Canon is, but the camera looks heavy, with a gigantic round lens that sticks out. I've never heard of a kid owning a fancy camera like this. "What kind of pictures do you take?" I ask.

"Literally everything." Olivia turns the camera carefully and shows me the small LCD screen in the back. "This is from our visit to the Seattle Zoo last month." She clicks through a ton of pictures: animals, flowers, the sky. There's even one of a sprinkler with water droplets suspended in the air like diamonds.

"These are all so good," I whisper-shout. "Totally professional!"

Olivia shrugs like she doesn't believe me. She's looking at a picture of a penguin standing on an ice cap. "Penguins are my favorite," she says, like she's trying to change the subject.

"You can't keep a penguin as a pet, though," I argue. "I'd rather have a dog."

She nods. "Dogs are pretty awesome too."

"Really?" I smile some more. "Which type is your favorite?"

By the time London comes back out with her Nintendo, Olivia and I are discussing different breeds of dogs and their levels of awesomeness. She thinks small dogs are the best because you can put them in your purse and carry them around like dolls. I think big dogs like Sir Teddy are way better because they can be your best friend.

"Dogs again?" London groans as she sits down next to us. She doesn't completely understand my dog obsession. Her whole family are cat people.

Olivia and I nod and giggle. "Yup," we say together.

London shakes her head and powers up her Nintendo. "Who wants to play first?" she offers, like always.

That's one of my favorite things about her. She's always happy sharing her stuff, even really special things like her video games. "Not me," I reply dreamily. "I'm thinking of real animals right now."

London starts a new game. "Have some patience, girl," she says. "I told you I'll think of something soon."

"Think of what?" Olivia asks.

I fill her in on the whole I'm-dying-for-a-dog situation. Olivia listens carefully, then says firmly, "London's right. We'll think of something together. That's what friends are for, isn't it?"

CHAPTER 3

The next morning, the three of us meet in the cul-de-sac again. I'd wanted to go to the park, but Olivia says her parents still aren't sure about the neighborhood. "It's okay," London says. "We can play hopscotch on the sidewalk." She's wearing a white linen jacket over her T-shirt today, the one that makes her look smart and cool.

I think hopscotch is babyish, but I don't say anything. London loves being in charge of our activities, and I'm fine with that. Having fun with friends is all that matters to me.

Olivia sits down on the sidewalk. She's got her camera with her again. "I'm going to take some pictures," she announces. London looks surprised for a minute. Then she shrugs and starts drawing squares on the sidewalk with chalk. I'm sure we'll all end up playing hopscotch when she's done. That's how it always is with London and me.

I sit down next to Olivia. "Any photos of dogs in there?" I ask, nodding to her camera.

"Sure," she replies, clicking for a minute until she finds one. "Meet my aunt's dog, Fifi."

I take a look at the screen and start laughing. It's a poofy white poodle wearing a tiara and ankle bracelets. "She's incredible!"

London comes over to peek at Fifi. "Imaan never met a dog she didn't love."

"That's true." I sigh happily. "They're all incredible, even those dressed like poodle queens!"

Olivia clicks to show me more pictures of Fifi. "If you love dogs so much, you should get a job working at an animal shelter or something," she says.

London and I exchange looks. Her mom actually does work at a shelter, as their business manager. We've asked a million times if we could get jobs there. But she keeps saying no. Apparently you need to be at least fourteen to work a real job.

"I'd rather have my own dog," I reply. "Who wants to take care of dogs you can't bring home?"

Olivia frowns at me. "I think taking care of animals is good practice. Like babysitting."

My eyes widen. "You mean pet sitting?" I ask.

"Exactly!" replies Olivia. "My aunt leaves Fifi with us when she has to travel for the weekend. It's a lot of fun."

My brain is whirling. Why have I never thought of this before? "That's it!" I whisper. "We could open a pet-sitting business! I bet lots of people do that."

Olivia claps her hands. "Perfect! Count me in."

London puts down her chalk and stares at us. "Start a business? What are you talking about?"

I turn to her. "It's not a real business. Just the three of us doing something together this summer. Might be fun, right?" I give her a pleading look.

"Okay," she says finally. "Tell me more."

Olivia and I say "Yay!" at the same time. That makes London roll her eyes.

"We could call it the Animal Club," Olivia says. "That way we can expand to other animals, like cats or hamsters, or even iguanas!"

"Iguanas?" I squeal. I am *so* not a fan of lizards.

She nods. "My cousin has a pet iguana named Rafael. He's really cool."

"Seriously?" I ask, trying not to feel jealous. Olivia

seems to have a lot of hands-on experience with animals, unlike me.

"I'm still not sure about this," London interrupts. "Pet sitting is hard work."

I cross my arms over my chest. "That's exactly the reason Mama won't let me keep a dog," I tell her. "Because she thinks I can't do the work. Maybe I need to prove to her that I'm responsible and caring. Maybe I need to take care of a few dogs to convince her I'm capable." I'm practically whining. London knows how much this means to me.

Her face softens. She leans over and gives me a hug. "You're right, of course."

We all stare at one another for a minute. Then our faces break out into the hugest grins. It's settled: We're going to open a pet-sitting business.

"So, names," Olivia reminds us. We huddle together and begin discussing more business names.

Some are weird, like Pooper Scoopers. Others are plain boring, like ABC Pet Care. I suggest Pawtastic, but London says it sounds like a TV show.

"What's better than an animal TV show?" I ask.

"The first rule of a company name is that it should reflect a story."

"What story?" I grumble. Where does she even learn stuff like that?

"Like why we created a company, what we want to do with it." She pauses, thinking. "Like our mission."

I think. Our mission. "Well, basically, we're three friends who want to work with animals, right?" I say slowly.

She nods. "Exactly."

For a while all three of us stare at the sidewalk under our shoes. Finally, Olivia snaps her fingers and says, "I know! How about Must Love Pets?"

London sits up. "OMG! That's perfect!"

I feel a happy bubbling in my chest. "Must Love Pets," I say. It really is perfect. I take a deep breath. "So, how do we get started?"

London writes something on the sidewalk with chalk. "First, we make flyers. Second, we post them all over the park. That's called advertising."

"Yes," Olivia says. "And we should get some testimonials. That means get some people to say how good we are."

"Like who? Our parents?" The bubbling in my chest turns heavy. I slump at the thought of Mama and her forty-three nos. "They'll never agree to this. Not in a million years."

"We still have to try," Olivia says, her eyes sparkling. "My mom says you never know until you try something."

Then I remember Dada Jee and his advice about making up your mind. If Mama gets mad, I could always say he's the one who told me to go after my passions.

"I agree," I say. London and Olivia grin at me.

We spend the morning making flyers on drawing paper London brings out from her house, along with a whole box of markers.

Must Love Pets. Best Pet Sitters in the Neighborhood! We'll Care for Your Pets Like They're Our Own. Call Us Today.

None of us have phones, so we use my home number. Mama never uses the home phone anyway, and I'm in charge of picking up the landline whenever it rings.

If anyone calls us, that is. Even though this was my idea, I'm not sure it will actually work.

"I took a break from work to bake some banana bread," Mama calls out from the kitchen when I get back home. I quickly stuff the flyers in the foyer table and walk into the kitchen like everything is fine.

"Mmmm, I love banana bread." I take a deep breath and settle on a chair at the kitchen table. There are already two pans of bread cooling on racks, and Mama's mixing a third batch of batter. I reach out to break off a piece of bread. "I love banana bread, Mama," I repeat, my eyes closed as I breathe in the smell.

Mama chuckles. "I know you do," she says. Then she raps my knuckles lightly with her spoon. "Just a piece, though. This isn't for you."

I open my eyes and pop the bread in my mouth before she can stop me. Delicious! "Who is it for, then?" I demand, eyeing the rest of the pan. "I'm your firstborn, Mother. The best daughter in the world. The one who keeps her room clean and doesn't mess up the house with toys and stuff. Who deserves this bread more than me?"

Mama gives me a stern look, but I can see that her lips are trying not to curve up into a smile. She secretly loves it when I get all dramatic. "Yes, you *are* the best daughter in the world," she agrees, patting my arm. "But this bread is for one of our neighbors, old Mr. Bajpai. He's recovering from the flu, and I wanted to help him feel better."

Mr. Bajpai is from India, and he sometimes comes over after dinner to play cards with Dada Jee. They talk in Hindi/Urdu and drink lots of lemonade from the lemons Dada Jee grows in our backyard. "Banana bread definitely makes people feel better," I agree, stealing another piece. Then I have another thought. "Wait, didn't you have some deadline? Why are you even here?"

Mama and her deadlines. I never thought counting numbers could be so . . . stressful. Right now, though, she looks relaxed, with flour on her cheek and the sleeves of her blouse rolled up. "I did, but this is also important, Imaan," she says. "Neighbors are like part of our big family. We should take care of them if they need something."

"Even if it's banana bread?"

"Especially if it's banana bread."

I watch as she pours the batter into a bread pan and puts it into the oven. She sets the timer and turns back to me. "That's the last one."

I wipe the smudge of flour from her cheek. "You go back to work," I tell her. "I'll take the bread out of the oven when it's done."

Her eyebrows rise. "You sure?"

"Yup." I grin. "You can reward me in bread."

CHAPTER 4

"Look, Imaan, I can jump so high!" Amir shouts at me even though I'm only two feet away. I send him a ferocious look. It's the next morning, bright and early. He's standing on the half wall that runs outside our house, arms outstretched like he's Superman or something.

"If you fall, I'm not coming to help."

He sticks his tongue out at me. "You have to. You're my big sister."

I turn away to my friends. "Nope, I don't have to." But I keep looking at him from the corner of my eye because he's fallen off that stupid wall before. It's not high enough for him to get really hurt, but he always screams like all his bones have broken from that little jump. Ugh.

"Ten, nine . . ." he starts counting. This will take a while because sometimes he forgets his numbers when he's going backward.

"He's definitely your brother," London giggles. "He's just as dramatic as you."

"I think he's adorable," Olivia says, snapping a picture of Amir. "I bet he lands a perfect jump."

I groan. "You're so optimistic. Have some more banana bread."

We're sitting on the sidewalk, chomping on the last pieces of bread that sit in the pan on the ground next to us. I begged Mama for it this morning, reminding her that welcoming Olivia's family was also an important part of our neighborly duties. She told me I could take a whole loaf if I also took Amir outside with me so she could work in peace.

I look down at the almost-empty pan. It was a good trade. I think.

"Get back to drawing, people!" London claps her hands. "We only have two more flyers left to make."

We now have twenty flyers full of color and art. And lots of exclamation points. I don't like the exclamation points too much, but London says they make us sound excited and happy to be taking care of people's pets. Olivia gets back to coloring with markers, but I can't really concentrate. "Three, two, one..." Amir's counting has become more like screaming. Then he shouts, "BLAST OFF!" and jumps.

I jump too, up from the sidewalk and toward that silly, annoying brother of mine. He lands on the ground, tumbles as expected, and then rolls down the little hilly slope of our front yard until he gets to the sidewalk right at Olivia's feet.

"See, perfect!" Olivia beams at him. "Good job, dude!" She snaps more pictures with her camera.

I rush over and pull him up. "Don't encourage him," I tell Olivia. "He could have been hurt. Mama would have been so mad at me. And then what would happen to my dream of becoming a dog owner?"

London snorts. "What did I tell you? Dramatic." But she's grinning, like that's the best thing about me.

I grin back. "You like me being so dramatic, though."

She throws a marker at me. "That is true." She turns to Olivia. "When we first became besties, Imaan would open her bedroom window and yell at me to come play with her. At the top of her lungs!"

I giggle. "How else can one communicate without phones?"

London is laughing too. "My mom used to get so mad at us shouting at each other from our windows!"

"Why did you stop?" Olivia asks.

I give my brother a sideways glance. "Amir got older, and I had to set a good example."

"Yeah," London says. "It was weird when he'd shout my name out the window for no reason. I mean, he's cute and all, but only my bestie gets to do weird stuff like that!"

Amir pumps his fists in the air. "I. Am. Awesome!" he yells.

I have to smile. His cheeks are red and his hair waves madly around his face like he's the cutest mop ever. "Okay, Superman. No more jumping."

He flops down next to Olivia and grabs the last piece of banana bread. "But I'm bored!"

London pushes the last flyer toward him. "Here, help us color."

I'm nervous because (a) his idea of art is scribbling all over the paper, and (b) he may tattle to Mama about this pet-sitting business before I can explain. But then I remember that he's six and isn't that good at reading big words yet. Still, I say, "Stay inside the lines," just to warn him that I'm his big sister.

"Yes, ma'am," he replies, and touches his forehead with two fingers like he's giving me a salute.

London and Olivia giggle as if he's hilarious. Their happiness is infectious, and I smile a little bit too. I guess Amir's okay. "Get to work, then," I tell him.

He takes the flyer from London and picks up a purple marker. I watch him color a cat, deciding not to ask him if he's ever seen a purple cat.

Amir only lasts ten minutes, though. Dada Jee

peeks out our front window and calls him in for a snack. "Later, alligators!" he shouts, and leaves.

Olivia sighs after him. "I wish I had a little brother."

I suddenly realize I know nothing about her family. "Are you an only child, like London?" I ask.

Olivia shakes her head like she's got some bad news. "Worse. I have a teenage brother, Jake. He's smelly and eats all the time. When he's not sleeping, that is."

I say, "At least he doesn't sneak into your room and sprinkle candy all over your clothes."

She shrugs. "I wouldn't mind. Jake hardly even talks to me."

London puts her flyer down with the others. "All finished," she says. "Where should we put them up?"

"We could staple them on trees," Olivia suggests. "My dad has one of those big staple guns."

"Good idea," London replies. "And we could drop off a few at Tasty."

Tasty is the little organic café at the end of our street. They make the best strawberry kiwi smoothies.

I'm just turning to Olivia to tell her all about Tasty when I hear barking coming from the street. I look around quickly. "Sir Teddy!" I cry. He runs up to us and licks us like we're old pals. His fur is soft against my arm, like a warm blanket I want to snuggle in.

I look around for Mrs. Jarrett. She's standing outside her house, looking at her phone. It's the first time I've seen her without a housecoat. She's wearing loose jeans and a long collared shirt that's not tucked in. I can see she's upset.

"Hello, girls," she calls out, as always. But her voice is shaky, like she's trying not to cry.

"What happened, Mrs. Jarrett?" I ask, grabbing

Sir Teddy's leash so he doesn't run all over the neighborhood.

"My mom's in the hospital," she replies, coming over to us. "She fell down and broke her hip, poor dear. I've been on the phone with doctors all morning."

We all make sad faces. Mrs. Jarrett's mom had come over for Christmas last year. She had wispy white hair tied in a bun and walked very slowly with one of those four-legged canes. "We're sorry," London says.

"I have to go be with her in the hospital for a couple days," Mrs. Jarrett continues, clutching her phone. "But I can't take Sir Teddy with me. I'm not sure what to do!"

I keep staring at Sir Teddy's leash in my right hand and a flyer in my left one. My brain's tingling like it's trying to give me a secret message. *BEST PET SITTERS IN THE NEIGHBORHOOD.*

"We can take care of Sir Teddy for you!" I blurt out.

Everyone turns to look at me. "You can?" Mrs. Jarrett looks 100 percent relieved. "Do you think your mom will be okay with that? She doesn't seem too fond of animals."

I nod quickly. I already know the answer to that. "Absolutely! We're neighbors, aren't we? We should help each other out."

London leans forward and hands Mrs. Jarrett one of our flyers. "And we won't even charge you. Just promise to give us a nice testimonial when you return."

Mrs. Jarrett takes the flyer and practically runs back toward her house. "Oh, this is fantastic!" she calls out. "Thank you, girls! Let me call my mother back and tell her the good news. Then I'll give Mrs. Bashir a call too!"

Olivia crouches down to take quick-fire pictures of Sir Teddy from different angles. London turns to me. "Are you sure about this, Imaan?" she whispers.

"Positive!" Sir Teddy sits with us like he knows exactly what's going on. I pet his head over and over, leaning my whole body against his warmth. "You're going to help me convince Mama I'm responsible enough for a dog!" I whisper to him. "She keeps saying no to me, but there's no way she can say no to a neighbor's emergency."

Sir Teddy licks my hand like he agrees with me perfectly.

CHAPTER 5

Mrs. Jarrett has already called Mama by the time we go into the house. Mama stands in the living room holding the phone to her ear, nodding and saying "mm-hmm" very softly. She doesn't look mad, but she definitely doesn't look happy either. All the while, London, Olivia, and I stand nearby, trying to act casual.

I can see Dada Jee and Amir in the backyard through the row of windows. Dada Jee is bent over his lemon trees, probably muttering to them like he always does. He calls them his babies, and I roll my eyes at him. I don't want him knowing how cute I think he is. Amir digs in his sandbox. He's all covered in sand. Ew. He isn't so cute right now.

"Hope he's gonna take a bath after that," Olivia whispers in my ear.

"Don't be too sure," I reply darkly.

Finally, Mama puts the phone down and looks at us carefully. "Mrs. Jarrett's mother is in the hospital," she says. Her tone is still soft, but there is zero softness on her face. I suddenly feel nervous.

"Yes, Mrs. Bashir," London replies, elbowing me.

"Yes, Mama," I agree. I wonder nervously how much Mrs. Jarrett has told Mama. Did she talk about the flyer and Must Love Pets? Did she ask about fees and testimonials?

Olivia nods, since she hasn't been introduced to Mama yet. Did we just get to meet her two days ago? I feel like I've known her forever.

Mama continues, "And apparently you girls offered to take care of her dog while she was gone." She narrows her eyes at me. "Is this another one of your big ideas, Imaan?"

"Yes, we offered." I pause, confused. "But it's not . . ."

London elbows me again. "We thought it was the right thing to do," she says, giving Mama a smile.

I nod quickly. "Mrs. Jarrett's our neighbor, right, Mama?" I say. "She was so upset about her mom, and she needed our help. We always help our neighbors. Isn't that what you said to me yesterday?"

Mama stares at me for the longest time. Then her face relaxes, and she slumps her shoulders a tiny bit. "You're right, of course. She was pretty upset on the phone too. And full of praise for you girls." Then she pauses, looking at Olivia. "You're the new girl, right?"

Olivia grins and waves. "I'm Olivia, Mrs. Bashir. Your banana bread was delicious!"

Mama smiles back. "Thank you. I hope you shared with your parents too."

Oops. We hadn't. I know Mama knows this too because her eyes are glittering with laughter now and she's looking at me in mock sternness. "Really, Imaan?"

I grin too because I know this thing with Sir Teddy will be okay. Mama has accepted defeat in the name of neighborly duties. I shiver with excitement. I can't wait to welcome Sir Teddy into our house. I can't wait to hug him and pretend that he's mine. Just for a few days. I shiver again and hop a little from the wave of feelings in my heart.

London pulls my arm. "Chill," she whispers in my ear.

I try to chill. "When is Mrs. Jarrett leaving?" I ask Mama.

"Right after lunch. She's packing now." Mama replies, then moves back to her laptop that's lying on the coffee table. She must have been working in here instead of in her office today.

"Wanna check out my room?" I ask Olivia. She nods eagerly, and London begins to lead the way like she lives here.

"Lunch is turkey sandwiches, and we have plenty!" Mama calls out absently.

I am *so* not a fan of turkey sandwiches. Still, I say, "Okay!" brightly, and follow my friends upstairs. Right now, I'll eat just about anything to keep Mama happy with me.

By the time I reach my room, London and Olivia have already made themselves right at home. London is lying on my bed, flipping through my copy of *A Wrinkle in Time*. "Are you reading this again?" she asks, raising her eyebrows. She's not a fan of sci-fi. She prefers fantasy, with magic schools and disappearing spells.

"What? I like it," I reply. I take the book from her and put it back on my bookshelf.

"How many times have you read it now, five?" she asks teasingly.

I shrug. More like ten. What can I say, it's my favorite book. Not just because of the galaxy-hopping travel, but mostly because Meg's looking for her father too, like me. Okay, I'm not exactly looking for Baba, but I like to imagine he's somewhere out in the galaxy, still alive.

Weird, I know. I've never told anyone why *A Wrinkle in Time* is my favorite book. Not even London. I don't think she'd understand.

I turn to Olivia, who's peering at a display of tiny plastic toys laid out on my dresser. There's a Smurf, a Snoopy dog, a train, a catapult, and a few other things.

"Are these from McDonald's?" she asks, horrified but also sort of fascinated.

I nod. "When my dad was alive, he loved taking me to McDonald's. We used to collect the Happy Meal toys. It was like our game." I pick up a red plastic convertible; it's got *Zahid Bashir* written on the side in black Sharpie. "I only kept the special ones, like this car that Baba said looked just like his first car when he started driving. A big piece of junk, he called it."

I stop because both London and Olivia are looking at me like I'm the saddest thing on the planet. It's how everyone looks at me when I start talking about my dad. I guess that's why I don't do it too much.

"I'm sorry about your dad," Olivia says awkwardly.

I shrug. "Thanks."

"How . . . ?" she asks, then stops. Her face is frozen, and her eyes are scrunched up like she's in pain. I try not to laugh. I've seen this exact face on so many people.

I know what she's asking, though. How did Baba die? "Cancer," I reply.

Her face crumples, so I pat her hand and give her a smile. "It's okay, it was a long time ago." I almost ask if she wants to see some videos of him Mama has saved on her laptop. They're happy family home videos, nothing scary or bad. Mama and Dada Jee get sad when I watch them, so I don't, unless I'm alone.

London sits up and claps her hands together so loudly, I jump. "Okay, new topic. We're getting our first customer this afternoon, so we need to get our act together."

Olivia sits cross-legged on my shaggy carpet while I sink down on my beanbag in the corner. No videos today. Like I told Olivia, it's okay.

"Remember that our job is to make the customer

happy," London continues. Besides reading fantasy, she also watches way too much *Shark Tank* in the evenings.

"Please!" I cry. "Sir Teddy is always happy to see us. He'll love staying with us, you'll see."

London gives me a look very much like our math teacher, Mr. Gordon, does when someone makes a joke in class. "Sir Teddy is not our customer, Imaan," she says. "Mrs. Jarrett is. And she needs to be sure we will take good care of her baby."

"We will," Olivia says. "I'll make a list of things we need to ask her before she leaves."

"Like what?" I ask.

"Like Sir Teddy's eating schedule, and how many treats he's allowed. It's important to keep the same routine as the owner so the pet doesn't get confused."

I'm impressed. Olivia wasn't joking earlier—she's a pro at pet sitting.

"Perfect," London says. "And I'll get Mrs. Jarrett's emergency contact information."

I lean back toward my desk and get some notepaper and pens. "Here, you can use these," I say, writing "Must Love Pets" on the top of each sheet and passing them around. "What should I do?"

London thinks for a minute. "I guess since you're the one who offered our services, you can be the comforter-in-charge."

I try to act like I know what she's talking about. I've watched a few episodes of *Shark Tank* with her, but I can't remember hearing that term. "Uh, sure, that sounds cool. What exactly . . ."

She smiles. "I made that up, silly. Just be extra nice to Mrs. Jarrett and assure her Sir Teddy is in good hands. Just . . . bring your best customer service game!"

I smile back, relaxing. "I know how to do that."

CHAPTER 6

Olivia goes back home for lunch, but London eats with us like she sometimes does on weekdays when her parents are at work. Amir is thankfully clean and very hungry, so there's no drama at the kitchen table. He's always quiet and adorable after a bath, as if the water has washed away all his energy for a little while.

We settle at the table, London reading over her notes like there's a test tomorrow. "Eat first, please," Mama says in a warning voice. There's a pile of turkey sandwiches on a platter, taunting me. I empty a huge packet of potato chips into a bowl and take a handful for myself. If I have to eat bland turkey, I might as well fill up with lots of chips too.

"How are your lemon trees today, Dada Jee?" London asks politely. I love that she also calls him my special name for grandfather.

Dada Jee is sprinkling chili flakes on his sandwich. "The lemons are growing bigger by the day," he replies proudly. "I'm harvesting them all week."

"I'm helping," says Amir.

I seriously doubt Amir is helping Dada Jee. More like dancing around in the backyard while Dada Jee picks his lemons. "We'll help you later, Dada Jee," I promise. It's not the first time London's done garden duty with me.

He grunts his thanks, then starts on a story about the trees he had in his gardens in Pakistan. "This American soil is nothing like the soil back home," he grumbles. "The lemons here are bitter half the time. I don't know why."

"But your lemonade always tastes delicious," London tells him, and he beams.

"Suck-up," I whisper.

Mama gives me a warning glance, but our doorbell rings before she can say anything. "That must be Mrs. Jarrett," London says, all businesslike. She stands up, straightens her jacket, and waves around her notepaper and pen. "I'm going to start the intake process."

I watch her leave with my mouth open. How does she know literally everything?

I stand up too. "I guess I'll go with her," I say to no one.

"Just a second, Imaan." It's Mama. She's looking at me with those hard eyes again. The ones she uses when I've purposefully forgotten an assignment or something. "What does she mean by 'intake process'?"

I try to smile. "Honestly, I have no clue."

Mama isn't satisfied. "When I spoke to Mrs. Jarrett on the phone, she said something about a flyer that you girls gave her? Called it a godsend or something. What's that all about?"

I gulp again, and the turkey feels like pebbles in my stomach. This is it. The moment of truth. I think of the forty-three nos she's already given me, and I almost break down. Then I think of Must Love Pets and how this is the perfect opportunity for me to be really responsible. *It's time to be brave, Imaan Bashir*, I tell myself.

"Here, you can see." I take a crumpled flyer out of my jeans pocket and hand it to her. It's one of the first ones, and we'd changed some of the wording after this, so it's basically trash now.

Mama stares at the flyer. "A pet-sitting business?" Her voice isn't soft anymore. It's loud and slightly panicked.

"It's just a summer project," I assure her.

Okay, that's not really a lie. That's exactly what it feels like in my heart: a very important summer project. I'm hoping that before the summer is over Mama will see how great I am at taking care of other people's pets. Then she'll definitely cave in and get me a dog.

Right now, though, she's looking at me like I've lost my marbles. "All three of you? Even the new girl?"

"Stop calling her that! Her name's Olivia," I cry. "And yes, all three of us."

She crosses her arms over her chest. "Really?"

"Really," I reply. "It's not a big deal. Olivia's done this a bunch of times with her aunt's dog, Fifi."

"Taking care of family pets is different . . ." Mama begins.

"Mama, please. We all love animals, and we thought it would be a good thing to spend time with other people's pets while being helpful. We'll share all the responsibilities. It'll be fun." I try to sound confident. "Besides, we've got London. She always knows what to do."

Dada Jee is looking at us with interest. "I don't think it's a bad idea," he says to Mama slowly. "It will keep the girls busy so I can take care of Amir. You know my old bones can't do too much."

Dada Jee loves talking about his old bones. Last week he knelt down to pick up something from the floor and then moaned for thirty minutes. I had to rub this gross-smelling ointment on his bare back. Ugh. Possibly my worst chore this year.

But his words make Mama relax a little. She

hands back the flyer with a sigh. "Okay, I guess we'll see how it goes with Mr. Ted."

I giggle. "His name is Sir Teddy, Mama!"

She shakes her head and starts toward the front door. "He may be nobility in England, but everyone's a commoner in America!"

Mama's wrong, of course. Sir Teddy is definitely royalty. When Mrs. Jarrett hands him over to us, she practically bows to him. "Don't you worry, Mommy will be back very soon," she whispers loudly in his ear. She's wearing a gray-and-black polka-dotted house-coat and looks really nice. Sir Teddy barks and wags his tail, then slobbers on her cheek with his tongue.

"I have all the information we need," Olivia announces, waving her paper in the air. She came back over when she saw Mrs. Jarrett outside our house.

Olivia turns to Mrs. Jarrett. "And you already have Mrs. Bashir's number in case you have any questions."

Mrs. Jarrett hands me a gray doggy bed and a tote bag that's so big I almost fall over. "Here are his bed, his food, and his toys. He doesn't eat in anything but his special Princess Di dog bowl, so make sure you use it."

Sir Teddy is grinning up at me, his pink tongue lolling out like he's super happy to see me. I have a feeling he'll eat in any old bowl as long as there's food in front of him. But I tuck the dog bed under my arm and pull the tote bag onto my shoulder. "Yes, ma'am," I say very politely. Then I remember London's instructions about customer service and add in my gushiest voice, "Please don't worry even a tiny bit. We're professionals. We're going to take fantastic care of Sir Teddy. Just focus on your mom."

London beams at me. Mrs. Jarrett beams at me. Olivia gives me a thumbs-up.

Mama just shakes her head. Maybe I gushed too much.

"Have a safe trip," she tells Mrs. Jarrett. "I'll text you tomorrow to give you an update on the dog."

I keep my lips zipped, not wanting to tell her that's the job of Must Love Pets employees. I'm also not sure you should be giving updates on animals you're pet sitting. Does a babysitter do that? Or my schoolteacher?

Hey, Mrs. Bashir, just calling to give you an update that Imaan finished all her assignments in the morning, ate 90 percent of her lunch, and used the hall pass once to go to the bathroom. Also, she's still not finished her science report even though she had two whole weeks for it. Can you please remind her again?

Yeah, we're not doing that.

I stand next to my friends, watching Mrs. Jarrett drive away. Sir Teddy's warm side touches mine, and he's panting hard. I hope he's not sad to see his mommy go.

I pat his head. "Don't worry, Sir Teddy. We're gonna have so much fun!"

CHAPTER 7

After Mrs. Jarrett leaves, Mama turns to us. "You girls better not mess this up," she warns. "And stay close to the house, please."

We're all nodding so much we probably look like bobblehead dolls. *There's no way we're going to mess anything up,* I tell myself. Pet sitting isn't rocket science. Kids do it all the time, just like Olivia with her aunt's poodle.

Right? Right.

Mama goes back inside the house, leaving the three of us on the sidewalk with Sir Teddy. We stand like statues. It's suddenly very quiet, except for the dog's panting. Plus, my heart is thumping really loudly, but I don't think anyone can hear it except me.

I stare at London and Olivia. They stare back at me with identical round eyes. I know exactly what they're thinking because I'm thinking it too. *So how do you actually run a pet-sitting business?*

I can't believe someone just drove away, leaving their precious pet with the three of us. We have absolutely zero experience taking care of large, panting animals with dozens of teeth. What are we supposed to do? How do we spend the next two days?

"Er, what do we do now?" I ask in a shaky voice. I clutch Sir Teddy's leash, and he nuzzles my hand.

Olivia quickly looks at the notepaper in her hand. "Let's see. Mrs. Jarrett said she didn't take him on his regular walk this morning, since she was on the phone with the hospital."

Sir Teddy barks like he knows exactly what *walk* means. Then he pulls against his leash like he's trying to escape.

I clutch the leash harder. I don't want him to run away five minutes after our business has officially begun. "Okay, so let's take him for a walk."

Olivia wrinkles her nose. "Where should we go? I don't really know where anything is yet."

"Perfect time to show you the neighborhood, then," London says, linking arms with her and leading the way. I know where we're headed. It's the same route London and I have taken hundreds of times, with and without our families. I tug at Sir Teddy's leash. "Walk, doggy?" I ask.

He barks madly and breaks out into a run. He pulls me so hard, my arm socket aches. "Ow, stop!" I screech.

Of course, he doesn't seem to know the word *stop*.

Why am I surprised? I half walk, half run after him as he heads down the street, ears flat on his cute head. "Will somebody help?" I call out, looking back at my friends.

Olivia whistles and claps her hands loudly. "Hey, Sir Teddy! No running on the road!" Her voice is big and strong, nothing like how she usually sounds.

"Olivia!" I say, shocked. I don't think shouting is part of good customer service.

"What?" She shrugs. "You have to be firm with animals."

She's right, of course. Sir Teddy comes to a halt at a stop sign and waits patiently for London and Olivia to catch up. We cross the road and continue down the street on the other side. *This is so nice,* I think. I could do this forever, just walk around with my friends and my dog without a worry in the world.

Not your dog, a voice in my head reminds me.

Dada Jee says that's your conscience. I'd like to ask who gave permission to my conscience to make an appearance inside my head whenever it wants.

Not your dog, the voice says again. Ugh, like I don't know already.

A few minutes later, Olivia turns to me. "Can I hold his leash?" she asks shyly.

I don't really want to give it up. But she's smiling and holding out her hand, so I nod. *It's okay*, I tell myself. *Sir Teddy belongs to all of us.*

Then I shake my head at my silliness, because Mrs. Jarrett is the rightful mommy to this big adorable creature. I hand over the leash, and Olivia starts skipping behind London. I jog a little until I'm close to Sir Teddy's other side. If I lean sideways, I can feel him panting happily against me.

That makes me happy too. No problem. I'll just ask for the leash back on the way home.

* * *

It takes us fifteen minutes to reach the end of the street. Not because it's so far, but because Sir Teddy stops every few minutes. Here are some of the reasons why:

A. He wants to smell some flowers in a yard.

B. He wants to smell some more flowers in another yard.

C. He wants to say hello to Mrs. Cohen's little Chihuahua, Kiki.

D. He wants to poop.

Okay, that last part is pretty gross. I suddenly understand why having pets may not be a perfectly amazing situation. All three of us stand awkwardly and try not to look down at Sir Teddy while he goes to the bathroom in the bushes. London is looking around like she's never seen this street before. I'm trying to take little breaths so I don't accidentally smell something that would make me want to puke. Olivia is the only one who's not acting weird. I'm once again reminded that she's been a pet sitter before.

I try to copy her. Eyes ahead. Foot tapping. Cool as a cucumber. She gives me a little grin, like she knows what I'm thinking.

I grin back.

"Woof!" Sir Teddy has finally finished and looks very proud of himself. Ew.

"Let's get out of here," London says.

"Wait," Olivia replies. "We can't just leave it there."

I don't have to ask what "it" means. She hands me back the leash, then finds some tissues in her jeans pocket and picks up Sir Teddy's poop very carefully. She doesn't even wrinkle her nose. Luckily, there's a trash can right next to us. She practically throws the tissues inside and says, "Run!" breathlessly.

I'm not sure why she says that. Maybe she wants to leave the memory of poop removal behind her. That makes total sense to me.

She starts to run. Then we all do. Sir Teddy is the fastest. I can barely hold on to his leash, but I manage. We're out of breath by the time we reach the end of the street. And we're all laughing so hard we have to double over and hold our tummies.

Inside, though, I'm a quivering mess. Do I have to be the official poop picker-upper if I convince Mama to let me have a dog? I mean, I'm sure it's no big deal. If Olivia can do it, so can I.

It'll just take some getting used to. And maybe a clothespin on my nose.

"Remind me to add one more thing to my intake list," London says, gasping next to me.

"What's that?" I ask.

"Plastic baggies for the next time we take the dog for a walk."

Thankfully, I don't have to reply because we've finally reached our destination. We all stop together; only Sir Teddy has to be pulled a little to make him stop. I look around with a sigh. This is my second favorite place in the neighborhood after the park.

"Welcome to Tasty, Olivia!" I cry, holding out my arms like I'm doing a little *ta-da!*

Sir Teddy gives a big, joyous bark. I guess he's familiar with this place too. It's the only restaurant I know where animals are allowed inside. I point to a sign on the door. "See, Teddy, it says all creatures welcome," I tell him. "That includes you!"

He barks again, his tongue hanging out like he can already taste the yummy delights sold inside.

London and I look at each other solemnly. Tasty is

our place, where we usually sit for hours just chatting. Sometimes after school we do our homework together here. That's why bringing Olivia here is a VERY BIG DEAL. This makes it official—she's definitely part of our group now.

CHAPTER 8

Olivia looks around the area where we're standing. It's a small group of shops at the intersection of our street and the bigger one leading outside the neighborhood. Besides Tasty, there's also a dentist's office and a pharmacy. It's not Walgreens or CVS, but a small one that also sells milk and veggies in case you need something in a hurry. I know this because Dada Jee often makes me run out and get something while he's cooking dinner. Mostly ginger or garlic. You can't make Pakistani food without those important elements, apparently.

Tasty's glass windows are covered with hand-painted art. There are pictures of ice-cream cones and lollipops, sandwiches and burgers. There's a pink-and-white-striped awning over our heads. "This place is cool," Olivia announces happily. "I can already tell."

"It's even better inside," London says, leading the way in. The bell tinkles when we enter.

"Welcome, friends!" calls out a familiar voice.

I wave to the lady behind the counter. She's tall and brown-haired, and she's wearing a pink-and-white-striped apron that says QUEEN OF THE KITCHEN. "Hello, Angie!" I yell back.

Technically, I should say Miss York, but she's told us a million times to call her by her first name. Mama thinks it's disrespectful. I think it's worse to not respect someone's wishes about their name.

Mama's name is Amna, but everyone calls her

Mrs. Bashir. Sometimes I wonder if she prefers that because it makes her feel closer to Baba.

Angie waves us over. "My favorite girls," she says. "And a new girl! And a dog!"

Olivia waves back shyly, saying, "Hi, I just moved here."

I point to a table at the front of the shop. "Why don't you sit down, and I'll pick out a smoothie for you. You can trust me. I know all the good flavors."

Olivia walks slowly to the table, looking around with wide eyes. "I wish I'd brought my camera," she says. I can tell she's fascinated with the shop.

I don't blame her. I remember the first time I walked into Tasty when it opened a few years ago. I stood with my mouth open for a long time, taking it all in. The bright red plastic seats. The wooden tables. The jukeboxes (I had to look up what those were: ancient musical devices that run on coins). Being in here is like being transported into one of those old movies that Dada Jee would've watched if he grew up in America instead of Pakistan.

"This is so cool," Olivia says loudly, sinking down on a chair.

London hands me some money from her pocket. "My usual, please!" she says, before joining Olivia at the front of the shop.

I smile. I don't mind getting her order. Mama's always telling me that doing small favors for other people is a good thing. It makes you a nice person.

I pull Sir Teddy over to the counter. He barks in excitement. Does he also have a "usual" at this shop? Mama's got an agreement with Angie, and I'm allowed to buy two smoothies per week from Tasty. Angie and Mama settle the money at the end of the month. London says it's called a tab.

I order strawberry kiwi smoothies for myself

and Olivia, and London's regular Berry Berry Wild. "How's your family?" Angie asks while she works at the blender. "Tell your granddad I want a batch of his wonderful lemons for a new flavor I'm trying out."

"Sure," I reply. "He's harvesting them this week."

Angie hands me a tray of drinks, then sits on the floor to hug Sir Teddy. He's in heaven. He pants and rolls around on the floor, showing his belly.

Angie laughs and scratches Sir Teddy's belly. "Doing some dog walking for this cutie, eh?"

I tell her about Mrs. Jarrett and her mom. Angie frowns a little. "I'm sorry to hear that," she murmurs. "Mrs. Jarrett is a darling."

"I know," I say. Then I take a deep breath and add, "My friends and I just started a pet-sitting business, so we're able to help her out."

"That's a great idea!" She gives Sir Teddy one last belly rub and then stands back up. After washing her hands at the little sink next to the counter, she brings out a brown bag. "Treats for my knight in shining armor," she says. "On the house."

Sir Teddy scrambles up, shakes himself, and barks about five hundred times. I'm guessing he knows what's in the bag.

"Good luck with your pet sitting," Angie tells me.

"Thanks," I reply. "We made some flyers. I'll bring them around next time, if that's okay?"

Angie points behind her, where a bulletin board full of all sorts of flyers takes up half the wall. "Absolutely!"

I lead Sir Teddy back to the table and hand over the smoothies. Sir Teddy is looking at me very expectantly, so I open up the bag and give him his treat. It's a giant dog biscuit in the shape of a bone. The way he starts chomping, it looks like it's his favorite thing in the world.

Olivia takes a sip of her smoothie with a dreamy look on her face. "Mmmm," she says. "This is perfect! I've never had kiwi before."

"Told ya," I reply, setting my glass carefully on the table and sliding in next to her. That's another cool thing about Tasty. They serve the food in real glasses and plates, not plastic ones. That way, you have to sit and enjoy what you bought instead of rushing out the door. I guess you can order to-go, but why would anyone want to do that?

London starts talking about kiwis and how they're very popular in Australia. I sip my smoothie and gaze at Sir Teddy lying at my feet, chewing on his bone with big white teeth. Everything about him is so perfect. No wonder Mrs. Jarrett treats him like royalty.

"Hey, Imaan. What do you think?" London waves her hand to get my attention.

I blink. "Yeah, kiwis are yummy," I reply.

Olivia cackles. "We stopped talking about kiwis a long time ago."

I drag my eyes away from the dog at my feet. "Sorry, what were you talking about?"

"The park," London tells me. "We're going to the park next."

Sir Teddy looks up from his bone and gives a tiny bark. Wow, this animal is a genius. He knows so many actual English words.

I wonder if Dada Jee can teach him any Urdu words. I only know the basics, like *haan* for "yes," and *nahi* for "no." Baby words, Dada Jee calls them.

I bet Sir Teddy can learn baby words in Urdu too. "Yes, you can," I croon to him, ruffling his ear. "Aren't you the smartest ever?"

London stands up. "Okay, I think the sugar in the

smoothie has gone to your head," she says. "Let's get moving."

Sir Teddy swallows the rest of his treat and gets up too. He knows exactly where we're going!

"Bye, girls," Angie calls out as we get ready to leave. "Bye, doggo!"

I take a very strong hold of his leash so Olivia or London won't get any ideas. I want to take Sir Teddy to the park. Me, Imaan Bashir, the best pet sitter—and soon-to-be dog owner.

CHAPTER 9

The neighborhood park is full of kids. London heads quickly toward our picnic table, but I say, "Wait, this is Sir Teddy's time!" It's true, this dog has a mind of his own when it comes to the park. He jumps and barks like he's eaten a bag of sugar.

Great. Now I'm wondering if I shouldn't have given him that Tasty treat. This pet sitting is hard work!

London slows down. Sir Teddy drags me toward a long, winding path at the edge of the park, near the fence. It leads away from the swings and jungle gym. Away from the little grassy area where kids play soccer. I think this is the path Mrs. Jarrett takes him on every day. He's so happy that I don't even mind that he's almost pulling my arm out of its socket again. "Slow down, monkey!" I tell him, laughing.

He barks to tell me he's not a monkey, thank you very much.

London and Olivia follow us. "Where's he going?" Olivia asks.

I shrug. It takes us another ten minutes to find out because Sir Teddy keeps stopping to smell things on the ground. A bush. An empty Coke can. A baby's shoe.

I worry that he'll need to poop again, but thankfully that doesn't happen.

Finally, I figure out where we're going. It's that big tree in the corner of the park, where we saw him a couple of days ago. As usual, there are several squirrels around. They chatter and run circles around us like they're teasing us.

Olivia giggles. "Look, that one's holding an apple core just like a human!"

Sir Teddy barks loudly, again and again. "Shh!" I tell him. He barks once more, then calms down a little. He stops and sniffs the ground again.

"Is he searching for something?" London asks, staring.

I'm not sure what's going on. I watch as he stops sniffing, then sits on the ground, like he's waiting for something. Or someone?

I wonder if he's missing Mrs. Jarrett. If I were in his place, I'd probably be wondering where my mommy disappeared to. What does he think of me, London, and Olivia? Does he feel sad or unhappy? Is he scared?

I hunch down next to him and pat his head. "It's okay, baby. Your mommy will be back soon. Don't worry."

He licks my hand. Then he puts his head on his paws and closes his eyes. I guess it's naptime.

London leads Olivia to our picnic table. Luckily, it's empty. "Come on, Imaan," she calls. "Let him rest for a while."

I tie Sir Teddy's leash against a low branch, then follow my friends. We all climb up on the picnic table facing the big tree. A few squirrels are running up and down, and one even tiptoes right up to Sir Teddy, but the big dog doesn't stir. He must really be tired. I sigh and lean back on my hands. I feel like curling down next to him and taking a nap too.

"So, this is your meeting place, huh?" Olivia asks, looking around. "It's nice."

London points to a fence close by. "There's Imaan's

house. You can see her granddad's lemon trees from here."

Olivia squints. "That's a lot of lemons," she says in a loud whisper, like she's shocked in a good way. Everyone thinks Dada Jee's only joking about his lemons, until they see those trees laden with hundreds of yellow fruit. They're like a mini-orchard in our backyard.

I nod wisely. "Those lemon trees are prizeworthy, you know."

Olivia's eyes get round. "Really?"

I giggle. "Not really. Just Dada Jee thinks so."

London smacks my arm lightly. "He's awesome, your granddad."

"You're just saying that because you like his cooking."

London grins and starts to describe all of Dada Jee's food creations. He's really not a great cook, but

Mama doesn't know any Pakistani dishes, so he ends up making things for us on the weekends. Things like korma (too spicy), and saag (yummy), and even biryani once in a while (heaven). Oh, and of course his special homemade lemonade.

"Can you please invite me to your house for dinner next weekend?" Olivia asks. She looks like she could be drooling.

I roll my eyes. "Sure." But secretly I'm pleased that my friends like my family's cooking. In first grade, a few kids made fun of me whenever I brought parathas for lunch, so I stopped. Mama explained a long time ago that some people think anyone who's different from them is inferior. I didn't know what *inferior* meant then, but I understood what she was saying. They were ignorant, Mama told me. Forget about them.

Now, in my favorite park, I look at London's and

Olivia's happy, eager faces as they talk about Pakistani food, and there's a glow in my heart. They are the complete opposite of ignorant.

There's a chatter next to us, and then a blur of brown fur. I blink. Next thing I know, Sir Teddy's woken up, and he's rushing to his feet like there's an emergency. "What on earth!" London yells. She flings a leg down, ready to jump off the table and go to Sir Teddy's rescue.

I put up a hand to stop her.

Sir Teddy isn't really freaking out. He's standing still now, gazing at a squirrel that's running around him in circles. It's brown, with perky ears and a small white streak on its head. "I saw this squirrel the other day too," I whisper. "I think they're friends."

"That's ridiculous," London whispers back. She doesn't like not knowing things.

Olivia sits up. "No, wait, I read stories like this in

a book once," she says. "A walrus and a duck became friends, and the walrus even saved the duck's babies from drowning. Animals can have friendships, just like humans."

I stare at the scene in front of me. It sure looks like friendship. The squirrel holds up an acorn in its little paws, and Sir Teddy sniffs it. Then he gives a soft little bark, like he's saying hello.

I knew it! This dog is a genius! "They're definitely friends," I say. My heart is exploding with happiness. How cute is this?

London leans forward. "The squirrel is pretty awesome too. Look at that white streak on its head. I've never seen a squirrel with these markings before."

"He's like Flash," says Olivia. "My brother, Jake, loves that comic."

I don't know much about Flash. Amir is only into Superman right now.

We watch the dog-and-squirrel show for a while. Flash chatters to Sir Teddy, then runs up and down the dog's back like it's a playground. Sir Teddy thinks it's hilarious. His tongue is lolling out, and he keeps moving around in a little dance.

Then a kid gets too close to us with his ball, and Flash scampers away with an angry squeal.

"Nooo!" Olivia moans. "Come back, little Flash!"

We wait for a few minutes, but Flash is gone. Sir Teddy barks, then looks around at us with big eyes. "Your friend's gone, buddy," I say, trying not to smile.

London gets down from the picnic table. "We gotta get going too," she says. "It's almost dinnertime."

Before I can move, Olivia runs down and grabs Sir Teddy's leash. "Come on, big boy! Time to head home!" she tells him happily.

He wags his tail, also happily. All of a sudden, my

smile vanishes and my stomach drops to the ground. I tell myself not to be silly. Olivia's allowed to walk him, just as much as I am.

Right?

Right.

CHAPTER 10

"So, where to now?"

We're standing on our street, just outside
the park. I turn and pull the gate firmly closed,
like I'm supposed to. The group of kids who
left before us didn't even bother with the
gate, and I'm a little bit mad at them. "You're
supposed to . . ." I start yelling, but they run away
so I stop.

I guess lots of things are making me annoyed
right now.

"Well?" Olivia asks again. She's holding Sir

Teddy's leash in one hand and waving in front of her with the other.

"What do you mean?" I ask grumpily.

"What do we do next? Where are we going?" she replies. "And why're you glaring at me?"

I swallow. "I'm not glaring. I just . . . I wanted to walk Sir Teddy."

She raises her eyebrows. "But you did earlier. Isn't it my turn now?"

"Well . . ."

She continues, "And London didn't get a turn at all."

I cross my arms over my chest. "London isn't even a dog person. She's got, like, a hundred cats."

London gives me a weird look. "A hundred, Imaan?"

"You know what I mean. Boots is equal to ten normal cats, at least."

"This is true," London replies, her lips turning up in a tiny smile. She fishes out her notepaper and pen. "Okay, let's make a plan."

"A plan for what?" I ask slowly.

"My mom says you have to have a plan when you're working with other people. Otherwise nobody knows what to do," she replies cheerfully.

Olivia leans to look at London's paper. "I already have Mrs. Jarrett's schedule for Sir Teddy. He eats at seven in the morning and seven at night. And he needs to go for a walk during the day."

Predictably, Sir Teddy barks at that. Apparently, dogs don't have great memories. "Shush, silly. We just came from a walk," I tell him.

He barks again.

London flips over her notepaper and starts making columns. "How about we divide duties, so each of us has a job with Sir Teddy?" She starts to write things like BREAKFAST, WALK, SNACKS, SLEEP TIME, and PLAYTIME. "Dogs love to sleep, so it's not like we'll need to be taking care of him constantly."

I bend down to rub Sir Teddy's head. "I don't mind playing constantly with this cutie pie," I croon.

Oliva reaches over and rubs another part of Sir Teddy's head. He turns and licks her nose. "Where will he sleep?" she asks.

London stops writing and looks up. Her face is frozen, like she can't believe she actually forgot something. "I . . . didn't think of that," she whispers.

"What's the big deal?" I ask, frowning.

Olivia says, "How will we decide where he spends the night? We only have him for two nights, and there are three of us."

Oh. I guess this is the wrong time to say he's staying at my place.

I mean, of course he is. I'm not exactly sure why Olivia and London are acting like this is a huge problem. "Well," I say carefully. "Mrs. Jarrett spoke to my mom, and she's the one who agreed to keep him, technically. Your parents don't even know about Must Love Pets yet. Right?"

There's a weird little silence. There are people around us on the street, but they feel really far away, like they're on TV and someone put the volume really low.

Then London nods slowly. "Right."

Olivia nods too. "That's a good point, Imaan." She stops rubbing Sir Teddy's head and slips her hand into her jeans pocket. He gives another bark, then settles on the ground with a yawn.

I sigh. "Okay, so problem solved."

London gives me a look I've never seen before, like she's not quite sure what to say. She bends her head over her notepaper. "Yeah," she mutters. "We just have to ask our parents and then we can decide where Sir Teddy sleeps."

Whoa. I did *not* see that coming.

I grit my teeth. For the first time in my life, I'm mad that London is so smart. Why does she get to keep Sir Teddy at all? This whole business was my idea. It's *my* home number on the flyers. Mrs. Jarrett called *my* mama, not London's or Olivia's parents. Sir Teddy lives next door to *me*, not the other girls.

But I can't say all that without sounding five years old. Ugh. I should have thought of a good plan for this pet-sitting business instead of leaving it all to London. I should have figured out how to keep Sir Teddy by myself, instead of including two other girls who are equally wild about animals.

Imaan, you're being selfish. It's that voice in my head. I ignore the voice, hoping it will stop whispering in my ear. It's perfectly okay to want something for yourself for once. I'm not being selfish.

Really? This time, the voice sounds like Baba. Not the way he sounds in Mama's videos, but the way he sounds in my memories. Calm. Soft. Questioning.

I close my eyes for a second. I have so many questions, but there's no one to ask. What if Sir Teddy loves Olivia or London more than me? What if he doesn't want to stay with me? How will I convince Mama that I'm a perfect dog owner if I can't make even one dog love me?

CHAPTER 11

I walk slowly to my house. There's a knot in my chest, which I try to dislodge by breathing deeply in and out. It doesn't work. Behind me, my two friends—and a dog—follow. I can literally hear their feet dragging behind me. Okay, not literally. But I can hear the silence like it's a real thing. I hope Mama's made something good for dinner. If I have to eat another turkey sandwich, I'll scream.

Of course, that's out of the question. Only Amir is allowed to scream without consequences.

"Stop scowling," London says, coming up next to

me. "We need to show a united front. For Sir Teddy's sake."

I scowl even more. United fronts are for soccer teams. Not neighbors fighting over a dog.

Especially not best friends slash pet-sitting business co-owners fighting over a customer.

The more I think about it, the worse I feel. And the more the knot in my chest squeezes my insides. Why had I ever thought pet sitting would make me the happiest person on the planet? We're basically all glum except for Sir Teddy, who's currently wagging his tail.

"My mom says if we scowl too much, our faces will stay like that forever," Olivia says kindly.

I wait for London to tell her that's not possible, but she doesn't. "She means wrinkles, I guess," London finally says.

Olivia stops at her house. The front door is wide

open, and lights are blazing inside. "How's the move coming along?" London asks her.

She shrugs. "Every room is full of boxes," she grumbles. "I have to sleep on the floor until tomorrow."

The knot in my chest loosens a little bit. That doesn't sound like fun at all. "Sorry," I mutter.

A teenage boy with floppy blond hair just like Olivia's comes out to the front porch. He's holding a phone in his hand. "Mom's been looking for you, O. Dinner's ready."

London and I look at each other. "O?" London says. "I think only Oprah's allowed that nickname."

"Good one," the boy replies, grinning.

Olivia's shoulders slump. "This is my brother, Jake," she mutters.

Jake waves at us. "Nice dog!"

"That's Sir Teddy," Olivia says. "We're taking care of him while his owner's out of town."

"Cool," he replies, looking down at his phone. "But you know he can't stay here, right? The house is a total mess. There's hardly room for us to walk around with all the boxes."

I sigh. I should be really happy with this development, but I can't. Olivia looks miserable. She leans down and gives Sir Teddy a hug. "Yeah, I know. Good night, Sir Teddy. Be a good boy!"

I don't even mind that he licks her like she's an ice-cream cone. "See you tomorrow morning, O!" I yell as she hands me the leash and walks into her house with Jake.

London and I head to my house. "You could have tried harder to look sad for her," London whispered.

"Shut up," I whisper back.

When we enter, I sniff. Smells like lasagna. Sir Teddy barks in approval. It's his dinnertime too.

Amir is jumping on the couch, watching TV. "Hi, Imaan!" he shrieks. "Hi, London!"

Sir Teddy pulls against his leash, and I let him loose. I guess he wants to investigate all the fun on the couch. Amir sees him and shrieks even louder. "Come, doggy! Come here!"

I shake my head. "No need to be so loud, Amir. Dogs have really good hearing."

Sir Teddy's tail is wagging so fast, you can hardly see it. Amir slides down the couch, and they start hugging each other like they're best friends.

London and I turn toward the kitchen. Mama's checking the oven, and I hug her. Dada Jee is standing at the counter, stirring sugar into a big glass jug of lemonade. "Ah, here come my testers! Come, I have a new batch of lemons you must try."

"Stay for dinner?" I ask London. I'm already feeling better with the thought of food inside me.

"Okay," she replies. She takes a glass from Dada Jee and sips.

"Well?" he asks eagerly.

"Delicious. And a little salty, maybe?"

"You've got a good sense of taste," he replies. "I've started adding a pinch of salt to the sugar. Makes the flavor profile more . . . complex."

"Stop watching so much Food Network, Dada Jee," I tease.

We get busy with dinner prep. Mama texts London's mom to make sure she can stay for dinner. I rummage through the bag Mrs. Jarrett left us to find Sir Teddy's Princess Di bowl. It's only when I've poured out his food and set it near the window that I realize the noise from the living room is off the charts.

Amir is yelling and running around in circles.

The TV blares a cartoon with rabbits running around in circles.

And Sir Teddy is . . . hyper. He's barking. He's jumping. He's panting.

"Quiet, please!" Mama calls. But of course, nobody listens.

"Amir, stop!" I yell.

He stops. But not because of me. He stops because he starts sneezing. "*Achoo! Achoo! Achoo!*"

"Cover your mouth, Amir," I tell him sternly. Seriously, this kid has zero manners.

"Can't stop!" he gasps between sneezes. Then he jumps up and down a few times for emphasis.

Mama and Dada Jee rush to him. "What happened, *jaan*?" Mama asks in an urgent voice. "Are you feeling sick?"

Dada Jee checks his forehead with a hand. "No fever."

"*Achoo! Achoo!*"

I stare at the three of them. They're standing

in the middle of the living room with freaked-out faces. Personally, I don't see what the big deal with sneezing is.

Dada Jee looks at his wristwatch. "Six minutes," he tells Mama. That stops me cold. *How long can someone sneeze without stopping?* I wonder. An hour? A day? Their whole life?

"Do you think it's because of Sir Teddy?" London whispers to me.

"Of course not," I whisper back. But actually, I'm not sure.

Mama is holding Amir in her arms, wiping his face and nose with a tissue. Poor guy. His face is red, and tears are falling down his cheeks. *"Achoo! Achoo!"*

"He's been fine all day," Dada Jee protests. "Not even a sniffle."

"Achoo!"

"I wonder if he's allergic to something," Mama finally says. "Like dogs."

I gulp and look around for the culprit. Sir Teddy has moved away from the action and is now curled up in the worst place he could have chosen: Dada Jee's armchair.

I gulp some more. This is bad. Dada Jee doesn't even allow Amir into his chair, and they're best buddies. "Sir Teddy, get down from the furniture," I whisper, hoping nobody else has noticed.

But, of course, now there's perfect silence in the room, except for Amir's sneezes. Dada Jee turns and looks at his chair. "What. Is. That. Dog. Doing. On. My. Chair?"

London tries to pull Sir Teddy's collar, but he doesn't budge. He doesn't even bring up his head from his paws. I guess he's taking his before-dinner nap or something.

Dada Jee is turning purple. "Get him off! I'll have to wash the chair cover now. This is unacceptable! In Pakistan, dogs don't come inside the house and sit on armchairs. Get him off right now!"

Mama hugs Amir harder, like she's trying to stop his sneezes with her body. "Imaan?" she asks, her voice strained. "What's your plan?"

My plan? I'm supposed to be the girl with a plan? Are you kidding me? That's always been London, with her notepaper and pens.

I look at my best friend wildly, and she sends me back that grim stare of hers. The one that means *I told you so.*

Then she says, "I guess it's time to ask my parents if Sir Teddy can stay with us."

CHAPTER 12

London is on the phone in my kitchen. I can hear her arguing loudly with her dad. I know it can't be her mom on the other end because nobody would dare argue with her mom. Mrs. Harrison is very strict. Cool, but strict.

No wonder she and Mama get along.

"But, Dad!" London moans. It's funny how she loses her know-it-all voice when she's talking to her parents.

There's more talking from the other end of the line. I try not to listen. My stomach is a jumble of nerves because even though I don't want Sir Teddy going anywhere, it seems like there may not be any other option.

Amir has finally stopped sneezing, but only because Mama took him up to his room. Dada Jee, on the other hand, is still here. He's standing in front of his beloved armchair, arms crossed in front of his chest, eyebrows like thunderclouds. Sir Teddy couldn't care less. He's lying in the exact same position on the armchair, only now he's snoring too.

I wish he'd stop snoring. It looks like he's teasing Dada Jee. Like he's saying, *This is my chair now. My spot to snooze. Not yours.*

Dada Jee gets the message loud and clear. "Imaan!" he growls. "Why is this animal still here?"

I look around desperately and spy a bowl on the floor. Of course! Sir Teddy's food. I grab a spoon from a kitchen drawer and tap it against the metal. "Sir Teddy!" I call out. "Dinner!"

It works. He opens his eyes, shoots off the armchair, and gallops toward me. The next second, he's got his head in the bowl, chomping away like he's starved.

Which he probably is, since we walked so much today.

I give his head a little pat. It's not his fault I don't know how to run a pet-sitting business.

Dada Jee groans in relief. Then he circles his armchair, staring at it like he doesn't know what to do next. "How do I clean this thing?" he mutters. "All the dog hairs. All the fleas."

I gasp. "Sir Teddy doesn't have fleas!"

Dada Jee turns his grumpy eyes to me. "How do you know? You're not a vet."

"He's not scratching at all!" I say. "I'm sure Mrs. Jarrett keeps him very clean."

"Hmph!"

"Ugh, I can't believe my dad!" London interrupts us, putting the phone down. "I guess I better go find my mom." Before I can stop her, she's pulling Sir Teddy away from his dog bowl. Away from me.

"London, stop!" I shout. "He's eating!"

Sir Teddy barks, but he follows London anyway. I notice that his bowl is almost empty.

Traitor. Did he already forget who just gave him dinner?

"Let me just take him to my mom," London says as she stomps out of the kitchen. "She'll be fine with it, I'm telling you. She loves animals. There's no way she's going to turn Sir Teddy away."

I start to panic. Everything London is saying is true. Her mom may be strict, but she loves animals more than anybody else I've ever seen. One time, we found an injured bird on the street, and she held it in her arms like it was a tiny baby. She even brought her lips to its beak and gave it CPR.

Right now, though, I wish she'd been a little less wonderful. I don't want her to take Sir Teddy in. I follow London and Sir Teddy outside. "But he should stay with me!" I wail. "Wasn't that the whole point of Must Love Pets? So that I can take care of a dog? So that I can prove I'm responsible?"

She turns, and that stern look is back on her face. "Imaan, you're being really selfish right now. Your brother is sneezing his cute little head off, and you're only thinking of yourself."

My shoulders slump until my head is almost touching my chest. Amir's teary eyes and red face fill my brain. I'd counted twenty-eight sneezes before Mama dragged Amir upstairs.

Is London right? Was the voice in my head right? Am I being selfish?

I watch her walk down the street to her house with Sir Teddy.

When I get back to the house, Mama is sitting alone at the kitchen table, eating lasagna. I remember she'd asked me earlier about my plan.

"London's gone to ask her mom if Sir Teddy can stay with them," I say in a very small voice. I know it's the right thing. But it still makes me mad.

She nods like she understands. "I think that's a good idea."

I don't. "How's Amir?" I ask, to change the subject.

She sighs. "He's better. I called the doctor, but I got the answering service. They'll call me back tomorrow morning."

I stare at the lasagna. I should probably eat some.

Otherwise, I'll regret it the next time Mama makes turkey sandwiches. But I can't. I'm so tired. And I'm already missing Sir Teddy.

Mama takes my arm and pulls me close in a sideways hug. "Hey, it's not your fault."

I blink. "Okay," I whisper.

"I'm proud of you, you know," she continues.

I frown. "Really? Why?" Making your little brother sneeze all his snot out isn't something to be proud of. Unless you're doing it on purpose to make a YouTube or TikTok video.

She lets me go and takes another bite of lasagna. "You offered to do something to help someone else, without any benefit to yourself. That's really good, *jaan*. How were you supposed to know that Amir would be allergic?"

"Or that Dada Jee would be so possessive about his chair?" I add, trying to smile.

Mama rolls her eyes. "Well, that part wasn't too shocking."

I stare at the table. "So, not selfish?" I whisper.

"No, of course not, silly." She pulls the dish of lasagna toward us. "Come on, let's get some food inside you."

I slide onto the chair next to her and watch as she serves me. It's nice to have her do these things for me sometimes, like I'm still a little kid. I have a sudden memory of Baba cutting up my food and feeding me. Did he really do that, or is it only my imagination?

I dig into the lasagna. "*So* good!" I mumble.

Mama smiles slightly. "Good food for a good girl, Imaan. Don't you forget it."

I gulp quickly. She's only saying that because she doesn't know the whole story of why I offered to help Mrs. Jarrett. Despite what she thinks, I wasn't being selfless. I was being the total opposite of that.

I should come clean. Keeping things from Mama never ends well.

But I don't say anything because the door bangs open right then, and London comes back inside with Sir Teddy. "Guess what," she growls. "My stupid cat, Boots, freaked out when she saw a dog. Like yowling-and-running-up-the-drapes freaked out."

I stand up. "What are you saying?" I ask, even though I can totally imagine Boots freaking. That cat is definitely a scary animal. Three months ago, I got too close to her, and she clawed me so hard I had to get a shot.

London is glaring at me like I'm the one who made Boots act so terrible. "We can't keep Sir Teddy," she replies, almost throwing the leash at me. "He has to stay with you."

CHAPTER 13

"*Woof!*" the dog says.

I lie on my bed and groan. "Yes, I know, Sir Teddy."

He's sprawled on his dog bed on top of the shaggy carpet in my room like he belongs there. Which is ridiculous, of course. He literally belongs in someone else's house.

"*Woof woof!*" he repeats.

I open one eye. "Quiet," I tell him. "I'm thinking."

He's a dog, so he doesn't ask me what I'm thinking. Dogs always know stuff, like when you're sad or happy or something else. Right now, for example, I'm both. I'm sad about the whole drama that happened at dinnertime. Amir's sneeze-athon. Dada Jee's grumpy, scowling face. Mama's look of disappointment. And finally, London storming away like she hates me.

But I'm also happy that there's a real live dog in my room. Lying on the floor at my feet, half asleep.

EEEP! It's an actual dream come true.

I open both eyes, then slide off the bed to my shaggy carpet to lie down next to Sir Teddy. He licks my cheek, and I don't even mind. I take a deep, deep breath. After a minute, the thoughts in my brain stop jumping around like they're on fire. The knot in my chest dissolves a little.

I should just enjoy this moment. That's what Dada Jee would tell me if he wasn't being so grumpy.

I look at the Happy Meal toys on my dresser. No, I decide. That's what Baba would tell me. He was always saying things like that.

Be happy, Imaan. Nothing is more important than happiness.

Ice cream is the best thing in the world. Did you know that?

Enjoy yourself. Don't worry about things.

Yeah, stuff like you'd find on a pillow in one of those home TV shows Mama watches on the weekend. I don't think anyone really believes it. But it looks nice.

Maybe Baba was a fan of home TV shows.

I think of my father and try to enjoy this moment. Baba's voice. Baba's laugh. Baba's smell, like pancakes and mint. It's weird how people don't want to talk about him to me, like he's a bad secret that will make me cry if I get to know it. I guess they don't realize that I like thinking about him. Talking about him. Keeping him alive in my mind.

Mama doesn't talk about him, ever. Dada Jee

sometimes mentions his name, then gets a grim look on his face like he ate something bad.

Amir, of course, doesn't even remember him.

Sir Teddy licks my arm, like he's saying, *It's okay, Imaan.*

There's a knock on my door. "Good night, Imaan," Mama calls out.

"Good night," I reply. Phew. She doesn't sound mad.

I look out my window. My room overlooks our backyard, which is right next to the narrow pathway leading to the neighborhood park, and beyond that the Harrisons' house. I'm too far up to see anything except the stars. But I know the park is there, with its tall trees and the playground. The picnic table where I sat with my old best friend and my new best friend.

London, Olivia, and Imaan.

Now it's only me. Imaan the All Alone, just like when Baba died.

The stars remind me of *A Wrinkle in Time*, so I gaze at them for the longest time. Imagining Baba hanging out in some faraway galaxy, chilling out, smiling. Sir Teddy whines softly, like he can feel my strange sad-happiness. I grip the fur on his neck and close my eyes.

My first sleepover with a dog, and I'm not even excited.

In the morning, things are much better. It's Saturday, for one, which means Mama's not working. More importantly, Amir isn't sneezing anymore, though his face is still red and splotchy. "I gave him a lot of Benadryl," Mama whispers when I get to the kitchen with Sir Teddy.

I look at Amir closely. Most kids get sleepy when they drink Benadryl. Not Amir. He gets even more hyper than usual. Right now, he's jumping from one foot to the other and flapping his arms around like a bird. His mouth is full of food.

"Hey, buddy," I say carefully. "How're you feeling?"

Amir stops jumping/flapping and turns around to stare at me. Then I realize he's staring at Sir Teddy right next to me.

Sir Teddy stares back. I'm proud of him for being so still. "Good boy," I whisper, putting a hand on his collar.

"I got sneezes from the dog," Amir tells me very seriously. "Eleventy thousand sneezes."

I clutch Sir Teddy's collar tighter. I'm hoping this allergic reaction is just a onetime thing, otherwise me getting a dog for real would be a big problem. "Well, we don't know that yet," I reply in a low voice. "You'd need to get checked out by a doctor to know that for sure. Maybe it was something else."

Mama gives me a scolding look from across the kitchen island. "It was definitely the dog, Imaan," she says. "And I don't think it should be in the kitchen right now."

I clutch harder. "His name is Sir Teddy," I say, louder this time. "And he's a boy. Not *it*."

I'm not sure why I'm being so stubborn. I know it's not a good idea to fight with Mama. She always wins.

Sir Teddy leans a little bit against my leg, like he knows I'm upset. The pressure makes me feel strong. I try again. "It's not Sir Teddy's fault even if Amir is allergic. He's a guest in our house. And I promised to take care of him."

Mama is irritated. I can tell from the way she's banging a spatula into a pan on the stove. She also looks super tired. Her eyes have big bags underneath, and her hair is a total mess. Not that I'll ever tell her that. One time, I told her she looked tired and she burst into tears. That was just before the tax deadline last year in April.

The tax deadline is evil. I'm sure of it.

Mama rubs her forehead. She opens her mouth to say something, then stops and puts the spatula away carefully. "How did you get to be so smart?" she asks me softly. "Of course it's not the dog . . . I mean Sir Teddy's fault. And we need to treat him well because he's our responsibility."

"Can I play with him?" Amir asks, stretching out a hand to touch Sir Teddy's head.

I pull the dog out of reach just in time. "No touching, just to be sure!"

Amir pouts and starts flapping his arms again. "That's not fair!" he shouts.

Sir Teddy barks like he agrees. "Quiet, Sir Teddy," I say. Then I squat next to Amir so I can look into his eyes. "You can play with him if you keep your distance."

Amir stops flapping. "What does that mean?"

"Like one whole arm away. And no touching. At all."

He thinks about it for a minute, then nods. "Okay! We can play hide-and-seek!"

I roll my eyes. "Sir Teddy can smell human beings from a mile away. Where do you think you'll hide?"

He's already running off. "Count to one hundred, Sir Teddy!"

"*Woof!*"

Mama walks over and gives me a hug. "Crisis averted," she whispers in my ear.

"That's me, Imaan the crisis averter." I spy the Princess Di dog bowl in the corner on the floor and remember that I have a job to do. Right now, I'm not just customer service but also operations control for Must Love Pets.

I imagine London's notepaper with her list of tasks. Bathroom first, then breakfast. I go to the patio door and open it to let Sir Teddy out. While he does his business, I fill his bowl with dog food, then get an old plastic container from the cabinet for water.

Mama is watching me with a little smile on her face. She looks . . . proud. I smile back. This is fun. I could totally do this every day.

Sir Teddy comes inside, tail wagging, and starts to chomp on his food like he's starving. My stomach rumbles too. Mama waves to the huge pile of pancakes on the island. "Will London and Olivia be joining us for breakfast?" she asks. "We have plenty."

Just like that, my smile disappears.

CHAPTER 14

Mama insists I call London's house. I don't want to, though, so I make an excuse and head outside with Sir Teddy. I can still see London's tight, angry face when she went home last night. I don't even get it. She knows the whole point of our pet-sitting business is to get me ready to be a dog owner for real. How can I do that if I don't keep Sir Teddy for at least twenty-four hours?

Maybe she got too attached. After all, anyone with a nightmare cat like Boots has to wonder what a dog would be like.

And Sir Teddy is adorable. A perfect pet, even if he does poop unexpectedly at the side of the road.

I sigh and pet his head. We sit down on the sidewalk in front of my house, where London's hopscotch lines are still visible. Lots of neighborhood kids are outside playing. Talking. Laughing. I probably look weird just sitting there on the side of the road, all serious.

All alone.

Ugh. Summer vacation is boring without your friends. London might be sitting on our picnic table in the park like always, but I'm not brave enough yet to go look. I lean forward and peek at Olivia's house. Nobody seems to be home. Or maybe they're all inside unpacking. I wish the door would open, even if it's just her brother with his phone. Maybe he'd tell me what to do.

But the door doesn't open. I feel like screaming.

Sir Teddy pushes his head against my leg like he wants something. "Wanna go for a walk?" I ask. Might as well get the checklist done.

Sir Teddy barks and scrambles to his feet. The kids on the street look at us. One of them points and waves.

I wave a limp hand. What if they think I stole Sir Teddy from Mrs. Jarrett?

You're being very silly, Imaan. Ugh, that voice. I suddenly don't care that it sounds like my father; it should just leave me alone.

Sir Teddy pulls against his leash, and I tell myself to stop thinking and start moving. Sir Teddy knows exactly where to go. We walk up the street just like we did yesterday. A few steps until we get to the stop sign, then wait and cross the road to the other side. He stops at the same places to smell the same flowers. Thankfully, I don't have to pick up any gross poop because he already used my backyard for his personal bathroom earlier in the morning.

Ew. This is one part of pet sitting I don't like.

The rest is pretty cool, though. I start having fun on our walk because it's just the two of us. Me and Sir Teddy. I tell him jokes, and he wags his tail like he totally understands them. I talk to him about Amir and Dada Jee and Mama. How they're so loud and annoying, but also the best.

Sir Teddy totally gets my whole family. He totally gets me.

We reach Tasty and go inside. Angie is busy with other customers, but her assistant helps me with a dog treat. Sir Teddy wags his tail even faster, and I laugh. I sit at a table toward the back of the café while he crunches on his treat, closing his eyes as if he's in heaven.

"The park?" I ask him when he's done.

"*Woof!*" is the very happy reply.

On the way to the park, I tell Sir Teddy about Baba. How he had black hair and brown eyes that always smiled, even when his mouth didn't. How his job was to fix people's computers. How he died from cancer in his brain when he was thirty-five years old. How I can't really remember him much anymore. And how I'm scared one day I'll forget all about him.

Sir Teddy understands everything. When I say, "Maybe we can watch Baba's videos together," he barks like he totally agrees.

I thought I was in love with Sir Teddy before, but I was wrong. Today, walking with him on the sidewalk, under a beautiful blue sky with puffy white clouds, is when I truly fall in love with him.

The park is less crowded today, maybe because

it's lunchtime by now. A few older kids are playing soccer in the clearing. One of them waves at me, and I squint. It's Olivia's brother, Jake. I wave back, then move ahead to sit at the picnic table. Sir Teddy settles down under the shade of the big oak tree. I search for squirrels, but Jake and his friends have probably scared them away with their shouts and kicks. Sir Teddy puts his head on his paws. I guess we're both waiting for our friends to show up, but they don't.

After lunch—leftover lasagna, thankfully—Dada Jee orders us to head outside. "We're going to spend the rest of the day in the backyard!" he announces, like *backyard* is code for Disneyland.

"Why?" I groan. I just want to curl up on the carpet in my room and read.

It's no use protesting, though. Mama's gone grocery shopping, so Dada Jee's in charge. And his rules must be followed even if they don't make sense.

He herds us all toward the back door. "There are many reasons," he says.

I let Sir Teddy go ahead, but I stand in the living room with my arms folded. "What are they?"

Dada Jee gives me a hard look. "One, the weather is good."

I peer outside at the sky. The sky is even bluer now, and the puffy clouds even puffier. Last weekend it rained constantly, so this is definitely a huge improvement. "Okay, what else?"

"Two, we have to entertain a six-year-old boy and a dog. It's safer to do that outside where they can't crash into things."

I think for a moment. He's right. Amir breaks at

least one thing in the house per week. Add Sir Teddy to the mix, and there's sure to be major damage. "Agreed. Anything else?"

Dada Jee's eyebrows meet in the middle of his forehead. "Most importantly, that dog can't get on my chair if he's outside."

I let out a laugh and grab Mama's phone from the counter. She usually doesn't leave home without it, but she wants me to update Mrs. Jarrett about Sir Teddy. "Okay, let's go outside, then!" I say.

Amir lets out a bloodcurdling yell and rushes past us. He's wearing his bathing suit and sunglasses, and he's holding a bucketful of plastic toys in his hand. "Come on, Sir Teddy!"

I shudder and follow him. "Sprinkler first?" I ask Dada Jee, and he nods.

The backyard is definitely not Disneyland, but

Amir and his new canine BFF are having a huge amount of fun. They run through the sprinkler and then waggle their butts to soak me with water.

I squeal, "Amir!"

"You have to come in, Imaan!" he yells back. "The water's awesome!"

"No, thanks," I reply. I sit on a patio chair and snap pictures on Mama's phone. I take lots of Amir and some of Sir Teddy. I even take one of Dada Jee in action as he shouts, "Don't get water on my pants, you rascals!" Then I search for Mrs. Jarrett's number and send her Sir Teddy's pictures with the caption "Having fun in the sun!"

She replies right away. *Thank you for being such good pet sitters!*

Pet sitters with an *s* at the end. As in plural.

I chew my lip, wondering if I should tell her I'm working alone today. Will she really care if London and Olivia aren't with me? All she wants is for her dog to be safe and happy, right?

Right.

My friends not talking to me isn't her problem. It's mine.

CHAPTER 15

"Come help me with my trees," Dada Jee says.

The sprinkler has been shut off, finally. Amir and Sir Teddy are lying on the grass, soaking up the sunshine. I've had to remind Amir three times about the arm distance, though. Seems like he's already forgotten about his sneeze attack the night before.

What can I say? Sir Teddy works his magic on everybody, even my annoying little brother with a nose full of snot.

"Your trees are fine, Dada Jee," I groan. But I still

go over to help him anyway. He's got six big lemon trees in a row, all green leaves and tall branches. Seriously, he treats these things better than real people. Polishing the leaves. Pruning the stems. Talking to them.

Weird.

Today, he's raking the ground around the trees and making it neat. Harvesting is still going on, which means wearing gloves, carefully taking lemons off their stems, and placing them *just so* in buckets. There are about five big, blue buckets lined up on the covered part of the patio, full of plump yellow lemons. "Are those for Angie?" I ask.

"Maybe," he replies.

"She was asking for more lemons," I inform him. "I think her Lemon Delight smoothies are a hit."

He smiles like he knows this already. Then

he points to Mama's phone sticking out from my jeans pocket. "Take some pictures. I'll send them to my cousins in Pakistan."

"Ooh, they'll be so jealous," I tease, taking out the phone and clicking.

He thinks I'm serious. "They won't. One of my cousins has a mango orchard in the village. My paltry lemon trees are nothing compared to that."

My hand freezes. Seriously? Dada Jee worries about somebody else being better than him too? I thought only kids do that. I give him a stern look. "Don't compare yourself to others! Isn't that what you always tell me?" I ask. "Follow your passion and all that?"

He goes back to raking. "Easy for you to say," he mutters.

"What's that supposed to mean?" I demand. Dada Jee is acting very strange today.

He clears his throat. "Your business. Pet sitting. It's a very good idea."

I've noticed that Dada Jee doesn't talk in long sentences. Short and grumpy, that's his style. For the first time, I wonder if it's because English is his second language. He took community college classes when he first moved to the United States. I know this because he still has the books in his room. They're little kid books, really, but they help people learn English. "What do you mean, Dada Jee?" I ask softly.

He doesn't turn to look at me. "You want a dog, but your mother won't let you get one. So, you've started this business as a way to convince her. That's very clever. Genius, really."

I'm so shocked I almost drop Mama's phone on the ground. I put it back into my pocket carefully. "How did you . . . ?"

He finally looks at me. "I'm your grandfather,

child," he replies, like that explains everything. "Don't worry, I'm not going to say anything to your mother."

I stare at him like I've never seen him before. "Promise?"

"Of course." Dada Jee ruffles the hair on my head and goes back to his work. After a minute, I get an empty bucket from the patio and sit on the grass next to him. With careful fingers I reach forward and pull a lemon off its stem. Then another. Then a third. It's actually very soothing. I wait for Dada Jee to remind me about gloves, but he doesn't say anything.

"It's no use anyway," I finally say stiffly. "The business isn't working out. My friends aren't even talking to me."

He grunts. "Your father was the same way. Always fighting with his friends, then coming home from school with the longest face you ever saw."

My jaw drops. Dada Jee hardly ever talks about

Baba. "Why . . . why did he fight with them?" I whisper.

Dada Jee shrugs. "Who knows? Someone cheated at cricket. Or got higher marks on the science test. Kids always have reasons to argue. You're not the only one, Imaan."

I want to know more. I want to know everything. I leave the lemons and turn to Dada Jee. Too late, because suddenly the backyard erupts in noise. *"Achoo! Achoo!"*

"Ugh, Amir!" I yell, standing up. "I told you, arm's length!"

Amir has totally forgotten all my instructions, of course. He's half sitting on top of Sir Teddy's back, laughing and sneezing. Between sneezes he shouts, "Look, Imaan. I'm on a horsey!"

"Get down, silly!"

And then something even worse happens. Like,

good and bad all mixed together. There's a chattering sound from our fence, the one that faces the park, followed by a blur of brown movement. I wouldn't even have noticed it except Sir Teddy goes nuts. He shakes Amir off his back and gallops to the fence, barking his head off.

"What on earth . . . ?" Dada Jee stands up slowly, squinting in the sun.

I look closer. The blur is a squirrel. And it's not just any squirrel. It's brown with a streak of white on its head.

It's Flash.

I take deep breaths. "It's okay, everyone. It's just Sir Teddy's BFF."

"Woof woof!"

"Achoo! Achoo!"

Dada Jee growls, "This BFF, what does it mean? Why do you kids always speak in letters?"

Flash is now on our grass, circling Sir Teddy like he's the most precious acorn. Sir Teddy barks for a few more seconds, then settles down on the grass too. I'm amazed at how gentle he is with everyone. Amir, me, and now Flash.

Flash doesn't get too close, though. He's jumping around, to the fence and back. Fence and back.

"*Achoo!*"

I realize Flash is scared because of my brother the sneeze monster. I grab Amir by the hand and pull him back toward the house. "But I want to see Sir Teddy's BFF!" Amir wails. Then he sneezes some more.

"Not right now," I reply firmly. "We need to get you inside."

What I don't say is that we need him to stop sneezing before Mama gets home. Otherwise, I'm toast.

Inside the house, I wet a clean kitchen towel and wipe Amir's face with it. Then I rummage through the medicine cabinet for Benadryl. He looks crushed and truly miserable, so I don't scold him for breaking the arm's length rule. Poor guy.

Also, poor Sir Teddy. I can see him from the window, waiting patiently for Flash to get close to him. Flash, however, is on the way to something very, very bad. He climbs back onto the fence, then takes quick steps toward Dada Jee. One, two, three, jump! Flash is now in one of the lemon trees.

Do squirrels like lemons? I have no idea.

All I know is, Dada Jee totally freaks out. He takes his cane and starts beating his trees lightly. *Slap slap slap.* "Get out of here, you squirrel!" he shouts. "My lemons won first prize at the Main Street farmers' market last year. Don't you dare get close to them!"

"His name's Flash!" I yell, but Dada Jee can't hear me.

Slap slap slap.

"Woof woof!"

"Achoo!"

Flash finally runs out of the trees, over the fence, and back into the park. Sir Teddy is heartbroken. He whines for a minute, then stands up and starts sniffing the ground all over the fence, like he wants to chase Flash and bring him back. Dada Jee isn't finished, though. He opens the gate in the fence and rushes outside into the street, waving his cane in the air like a thin gray weapon. "Don't come back here!" he shouts again. "I don't care what BFF means, just don't come back to my lemon trees!"

Amir tugs at my hand. I think the Benadryl is working because he's stopped sneezing. "I'm hungry, Imaan," he says in a low voice, rubbing his red eyes.

I heave a huge sigh. This is all my fault. Not just his cute, itchy face but also the drama outside.

"How about we eat some gooey mac 'n' cheese?" I ask miserably.

He cheers up immediately. "Great idea. Cheese makes everything better!"

I wish *my* life were that simple.

CHAPTER 16

I don't think about Sir Teddy for the next half hour.

This should tell you how much my mind is messed up, because for so many months, a dog has *always* been in my thoughts. Like, constantly. Today, though, after everything that's happened, I kick all thoughts of pets from my mind. It's like that yoga video Mama sometimes watches on the weekends. *Clear all impulses from your consciousness. Clear your needs, your wants. Your worldly desires.*

Maybe I should try yoga. It has to be way easier

than pet sitting. And baby brother sitting. And angry grandfather sitting.

Of course, I don't stop thinking of Sir Teddy on purpose. That would be awful, and very irresponsible. But that's what happens because I'm so busy thinking about other things. I'm watching Amir for more signs of allergy. I'm making a pot of mac 'n' cheese and praying I don't burn it. I'm heating up some frozen breadsticks in the oven. I'm trying to ignore Dada Jee as he paces up and down the living room, muttering about stupid squirrels and hyperactive dogs, and the state of wildlife in America overall. I'm eyeing the home phone in the hallway, wondering if I should call London and beg her forgiveness.

London, please come help me. Please be my friend again. I miss you. I'm sorry.

Mama's cell phone rings, making me jump. It's the doctor's office, asking Amir to come in next week for an allergy test. I write down the details on the note-pad on the counter, then send up a little prayer that the test comes out negative for dogs. Otherwise, I can kiss my dreams of dog ownership good-bye forever.

I've just put the phone down when the oven dings. I pull on an oven mitt and take out the breadsticks. They probably smell heavenly, but I don't really notice. The mac 'n' cheese on the stove bubbles, all gooey and golden, and I quickly take it off the stove. It's a miracle! I actually cooked it perfectly. I put some on a plate for Amir, saying, "Careful, it's hot!" so he doesn't start yelling when he takes a bite.

He takes a bite and yells, "Ow, it's hot!"

I glare at him. "Seriously?"

He blows on the mac 'n' cheese like it's a birth-day cake, and his spit flies around. Gross. I step away from the table and call out to Dada Jee. "Come eat, Dada Jee!"

He stops pacing and gives me a look. "No, absolutely not! If I leave this room, that dog of yours will climb up on my armchair again. Not on my watch!"

I roll my eyes. "He won't. He's not even here, see?"

And that's when I realize what I just said. *He's not even here.*

"What's happened?" Dada Jee asks. He's noticed my suddenly panicked expression, no doubt.

I look around frantically. "Where's Sir Teddy?" It takes all of two seconds to scan the entire kitchen/living room space and realize he's not here. Maybe he went upstairs to my room. Or the bathroom. Dogs love drinking from the toilet, don't they?

Actually, I have no idea about this. I saw it on a TV show once. I really hope he's not drinking from the toilet.

I rush around the house like I'm participating in

one of Amir's insanely fast hide-and-seek games. The one with a timer, where you have to find everyone as quickly as possible or you lose.

Spoiler alert: I never win those things.

But today, I have to win. I'm sure he's right here, I tell myself. I just *have* to find him. "It's fine, I'm sure it's fine," I say, panting. But honestly, I'm not really sure. He's not in my bedroom. Or in any other room. Not even the bathrooms.

I check every space in the entire house. I check under all the beds, even though he's too big to crawl that low. Amir has slid off his chair and started following me, holding a piece of breadstick in his hand like a treat. "Hey, doggy!" he keeps shouting. "I got something for you!"

I think about telling Amir that bread isn't good for dogs, but then I see him taking bites out of the breadstick, so I decide it doesn't really matter. He'll probably finish all of it before we find Sir Teddy.

"Here, doggy!" Amir calls again, holding out an oily hand.

"Remember not to touch him, okay?!" I say, looking back at Amir.

Of course, Amir doesn't answer. Amir always does exactly as he wants.

When we've searched the entire house (including the garage, even though there's no way Sir Teddy could have opened that locked door by himself), we go back to the living room with heavy steps. Amir licks his hands, but I don't care. I'm too tired and scared.

Dada Jee is still standing in the same spot, hands on hips. Only now he's looking out the windows. Is he staring at his lemon tree again? Does he care that I can't find Sir Teddy? Surely animals are more important than plants, right?

I don't ask him this last question because I'm worried I won't like his answer too much.

Amir flops down on the couch. I sink down too, totally exhausted. "He's not in the house," I mumble.

No reply from Dada Jee. He's still looking outside, his face frozen like he's a very wrinkled statue.

Wait a minute. Outside! The last time I'd seen Sir Teddy was in the backyard, reuniting with his BFF Flash. Then Amir had started sneezing and I'd dragged him into the house. I jump up from the couch and rush outside. Okay. Phew. Sir Teddy's probably sleeping under the shade of some trees, unaware of the fuss inside.

But nope. The backyard is completely empty. No Sir Teddy. No Flash. Not even a single bird. The yard looks just like always. Green grass. Lemon trees. Sprinkler.

Then I look closer. Guess what. One thing is very different. And very wrong.

The gate in the fence, the one that leads out to the street, is wide open.

I stare at it with panicked eyes. No, it can't be! I remember Dada Jee opening the gate and chasing Flash out of the yard. I remember him yelling and shaking his cane over his head.

I walk back slowly and stand on the edge of the patio, peering into the living room. "Dada Jee, did you bring him in?" I call, my voice shaking.

"I can't hear you, girl." He takes forever to walk to me, but finally he joins me on the patio, hands on hips. "What did you say?"

I repeat the question very slowly. "Did you bring Sir Teddy inside when you came in?"

Dada Jee's scowl is ferocious. "Why would I do that? I'm not his pet sitter. *You* are. It's *your* job."

My heart is literally jumping around in my chest like it's a wild creature. "I was looking after Amir!" I yell, even though you're not supposed to raise your voice to your elders. "He was sneezing, remember?"

"And I was trying to get that squirrel away from my lemons!" he replies, but he's lost the scowl. His shoulders slump. "I didn't even think of the dog," he whispers.

But he's trying to think now; I can tell because his face is totally horrified. We're both staring at the open gate like it's a ghost.

Amir is the one who bursts our silent bubble. "I think Sir Teddy escaped," he offers cheerfully. "That's what I'd do, anyway, if no one was watching me."

CHAPTER 17

It's official. I'm a failure. I lost my first pet on the first job I ever got. And Sir Teddy wasn't just a client's dog. He was so special. We understood each other! Now he's on the loose, lost in the vast jungle of our neighborhood. Mrs. Jarrett will actually kill me.

"Nobody's killing anyone, Imaan," Mama says.

She's back from the grocery store, emptying groceries from the bag onto the kitchen counter. I sit at the table, my head bowed, trying not to cry. I always help her with the groceries, but this time I can't even move.

I rub my eyes. "What part of 'lost forever' don't you understand?" I moan. I tell myself that I should resign from Must Love Pets. I should just accept defeat. Nobody will let me take care of their animal once the news gets out. My reputation will be destroyed.

"You're too dramatic for your own good," Mama tells me. "Instead of doing something, you're just sitting here moaning."

I'm about to tell her that I went out to the street but it was absolutely, completely empty. Even the kids who play outside weren't there. But then I focus on what she's saying. Dramatic? That's London's word for me.

London! I can't believe I've forgotten my best friend. The smartest person in fifth grade. She'll know what to do.

I jump up, shouting, "Of course!" and rush out of the house.

"See, so dramatic!" Mama calls out behind me.

I don't care. They can call me Dramatic Bashir from now on. I know my friends will help me. We created Must Love Pets together; our friendship story is literally in the company name. I'm not in this alone. I get to London's front door, take a deep breath, and start banging.

She opens the door like she's been waiting for me. "What?" she says, her face annoyed. She's wearing her jacket, which is a good sign. It means she's ready to get to work.

"Sir Teddy's missing," I say, panting. "He escaped from our backyard. I need your help!"

For a second she stares at me, and I wonder if she'll say no. Then her face changes to worry, and she pushes past me like a hurricane. "We need to have a staff meeting," she tells me, running to Olivia's house next door. In a minute, Olivia is outside too, camera in hand, and we huddle together on her porch.

"Tell us everything," London commands.

I tell them the whole story. Dada Jee's obsession with his lemon trees. Playing in the sprinkler. Flash making a guest appearance in our backyard. The search for Sir Teddy through my house and then finding the gate open. My voice is shaky, and I can feel tears building up behind my eyelids. "It wasn't your fault," London says when I stop talking.

I shake my head. "It doesn't matter. He was my responsibility, and I didn't do a good job."

"Well, technically," Olivia says in a small voice, "he was *our* responsibility. And we left you alone with him."

London nods. "None of us did a good job," she says. "I'm sorry, Imaan."

Olivia's head bobs up and down. "Me too."

"Thanks." I sigh. My eyes are totally blurry with tears now. Not a good look. I hang my head in misery. "What do we do?"

There's a little silence, then I feel arms all around my body. I look up. London is hugging me from one side, and Olivia from the other. London's head is pressed to mine. "It's okay, silly. I've got a plan."

The plan apparently involves the whole entire neighborhood. We knock on every single door on our street, asking if anybody has seen Sir Teddy. Most people say no. Mr. Bajpai says he doesn't even know who Mrs. Jarrett is, let alone that she owns an escape artist–type dog. "Tell your grandfather I'm coming over next weekend to play cards," he tells me, coughing.

"Hope you feel better soon," I mumble, wondering if he realizes you're not supposed to visit people if you have the flu. Maybe he thinks he'll be all better by next weekend.

When we get to the last door on the street, we finally have some luck. A group of teenagers opens the door, laughing and talking about some video game marathon. My eyes pop because one of the teens is Olivia's brother, Jake. "Oh yeah, I remember that dog from the park—he was really cool," he says, grinning at us.

"Did you see him again?" I ask hopefully.

He thinks for a moment. "When I was headed back home, I think I saw the dog running down the street." He squints and points away from my house, to the stop sign. "That way."

I blink. "Wait, you saw a dog running away alone and didn't tell anyone?"

Olivia groaned. "He's always like this," she tells us.

Jake shrugs. "I was thinking about soccer. It was a really intense game."

London puts a hand on my arm to stop me from freaking out. "That's where we walked yesterday," she says, looking to the stop sign.

I turn to London. "And today too," I admit. "I took him for another walk this morning, and we went the same route."

Olivia claps her hands. "Maybe he's following the route, like it's a game or something."

We start half running on the sidewalk. "Wait," Jake calls after us. "I feel bad. Can I help?"

"Sure," I reply, even though I'm not sure what he can do.

He pulls out his phone. I wonder why he offered to help if he can't even stop his video games for a little while. But soon, I get a surprise. Other kids his age start streaming out of their houses up and down the street, nodding and giving one another high fives. The soccer team, apparently.

London grins like this is the best thing to happen. "Okay, people! Here's the plan!" she shouts, waving her arms about like she's directing traffic. She's so good at being a leader. She takes Olivia's camera and shows everyone a picture of Sir Teddy. Then she assigns everyone jobs. I bet if she had a whistle, she'd be blowing into it like our P.E. coach.

By now, a couple of adults have also joined us. London is being so awesome, even the grown-ups listen carefully and follow her lead. I'm so proud of her.

"Let's go find Sir Teddy!" she orders.

Then we're off. London, Olivia, and I walk briskly down the main street, arms linked together. Jake follows us, even though Olivia gives him another dirty look. "I have a phone, it might be helpful," he tells her.

London pulls Olivia away. "He's right. We may need him."

A few kids go onto the side streets. The adults start to knock on doors ahead of us, asking questions. The rest of the search party follows us. I see movement nearby and turn my head slightly. It's Dada Jee, muttering, poking his cane in plants and hedges around him. I guess he feels bad about letting Sir Teddy out accidentally. I give him a little wave, trying to smile even though the knot in my chest is tighter than it's ever been before.

He waves back, and from his face it's obvious he's got the knot too.

Olivia, London, and me—plus Jake—continue down the street, shouting, "Sir Teddy! Where are you?" every few minutes. We pass by the flowers he always sniffs. Olivia points. "Look, they're flattened, like something big stepped on them."

Farther up is the place where Sir Teddy pooped the first day. The trash can is toppled over, like someone pushed it.

"What if he didn't even come in this direction?" I say, biting my lip. I try not to think of him lost and alone, wondering where everyone is. Poor baby.

Olivia squeezes my hand. "We have to keep trying, though."

I know she's right. I shouldn't admit defeat just yet. We walk on, and soon we're at the end of the neighborhood in the little shopping center with Tasty.

Angie's standing outside, waving at us. "Thank goodness you're here!"

CHAPTER 18

Angie talks to us outside her café, looking at our impromptu search party with wide eyes. "Sir Teddy was just here, I swear!" she tells us, breathless. "I gave him a treat and told him to sit in the corner until I finished serving my customers."

London snaps her fingers. "I knew it!" she exclaims. "He was following our route! The next stop was Tasty, of course!"

"And his favorite treat!" Olivia agrees.

My heart thumps in my chest with disappointment. I was so sure we'd find Sir Teddy safe and sound with

Angie. A little sob escapes my throat, and my friends turn to look at me.

"It's okay, Imaan," London tells me. "Just breathe."

I gulp air into my lungs and tell myself she's right. All businesses face problems, especially in the beginning. No need to panic.

Angie is wringing her hands. "I feel so bad. I should have called your mom right away," she says. "To be honest, I wasn't sure what the situation was. I thought he was on his walk, so I waited for a few minutes, thinking one of you girls would show up. Then I suddenly got a line of customers in the door." She sighs. "I thought it wouldn't hurt to serve them first."

I take another deep, steadying breath. "Of course. This is your store. Customer service is always top priority."

London chuckles a little, even though she

looks worried. "Glad to hear you remember that."

I try to smile back. "I was taught by a master."

The rest of the crowd is starting to get restless. Jake steps forward, his phone in his hand. "The kids have checked the whole neighborhood," he says. "No sign of the target."

Olivia shakes her head. "Target? This isn't some video game, you know."

His face turns red. "I know. Sorry, I meant Sir Teddy."

Everyone looks at London like they're expecting her to solve this problem I've created. She swallows, and I can see her throat move.

I know why she's so nervous. Just ahead of us is the big intersection, with the road that leads outside the neighborhood.

If Sir Teddy's gone in that direction, we may never find him.

I can't bear to think of Mrs. Jarrett's face when she finds out.

There's also another thing. If we lose Sir Teddy, I'll be a total failure as a pet sitter, and Mama will never, ever let me have a dog.

I breathe deeply again. In and out. All I have to do is prove I'm not a total failure. Right? Right.

Dada Jee's standing close by with anxious eyes. I think of what he always says: *Making up your mind is the first step to achieving something.* Well, we have something to achieve here, don't we?

I square my shoulders and turn back to London. "So, if this is a route Sir Teddy's following, we have to think of why."

London's forehead wrinkles. "He had fun with us. And we walked this way to get his treat, so that's a reward."

Olivia brightens up. "Dogs love rewards. That's how you train them, right?"

"Right," London replies. "That means we have to keep following the reward trail. What's the next thing he'd want to do after getting a Tasty treat? Where did we go next?"

I'm already walking. "The park!" I yell.

We move in a crowd toward the neighborhood park. It's almost dusk now, and the sun is low on the horizon. I break into a run. Once it gets dark, our chances of finding him will be even lower.

We circle back to our street and pass by my house. Mama is standing in the driveway, talking on her phone, with London's mom next to her. I really hope they're not talking to Mrs. Jarrett. The next minute, I reach the neighborhood park and screech to a halt outside the gate. It's supposed to be locked, but when I put out a hand to the keypad to punch in the code, the gate swings open.

"Stupid kids," I hear Dada Jee mutter right behind me.

But suddenly I think it's a good thing someone left the door open. That means maybe—just maybe—Sir Teddy got inside. I stare at the keypad as if there's some answer written on it. *Yes, he's got to be in there, it's our favorite place,* the voice in my head whispers. Is it my conscience? Or Baba? I shake my head to clear it.

"What are you waiting for?" Jake calls out.

I turn around to face the crowd. "If we all rush in, we could scare him."

London gives me an impatient look. "We don't even know if he's in there yet, Imaan!"

"Let me go in first," I say, more firmly this time. "Just to look around."

She stares at me. I stare back. Finally, she sighs. "Okay, fine. We'll wait here."

Jake starts waving his arms about. "Okay, people! Let's spread out and take one last look in the side streets. We may have missed something!"

The crowd starts to disperse. A few of the younger kids are obviously tired, and they sit down on the sidewalk and start talking quietly. This will definitely be a summer memory for years to come: the time we all looked for a lost dog like in the movies.

I take a deep breath and slip inside the park. It's weird this time of day, with the sun hidden almost completely behind the trees, and the birds all making loud, shrieking sounds as they settle into their nests for the night. The sky is purple, and I have to stare ahead to pick out the path Sir Teddy and I walked on.

I wasn't really being honest with everyone back there. I didn't want to go inside alone because a crowd would scare Sir Teddy. I didn't even want to do this alone because I felt responsible. Okay, that was part of the reason. But the real reason was something else. The real reason was that I didn't want everyone to see my face if he wasn't even here. If we searched the whole park and didn't find Sir Teddy, that would mean we failed. I failed. It would mean Must Love Pets was over before it even started properly.

And I know my face would look . . . bad. Sad and terrified and totally crushed.

Just like when Baba died.

And I know from experience that nobody wants to see that face. People get all uncomfortable when they see you upset at losing something very special. They shuffle their feet and clear their throats and look away. And I hate it.

So, it's better to go in alone. That way, in case Sir Teddy isn't here, I can let my emotions show on my face for just a minute without worrying anyone.

I take a deep breath. Okay, showtime. I don't even look around the park as I jog toward the back. I head straight to the picnic tables and the big tree. Sir Teddy and Flash's tree. It takes me all of two minutes to get there.

I'm breathing fast by the time I get there. And then I have to stop and take another deep, deep breath, because OMG.

Sir Teddy's sitting there like he doesn't have a single care in the world! Actually, he's lying there, with his head on his paws, eyes closed. Flash, that BFF of his, is sitting all curled up on his back.

Unbelievable! Even though I suspected I'd find him here, I'm still shocked. "Sir Teddy!" I gasp, trying to get my breathing under control.

He opens his eyes and stands up slowly so Flash has time to slide off his back.

I walk up to them and stand there, hands on

hips, trying to look mad. "You silly dog! You scared everyone!"

Flash chatters happily and scampers up a tree. Sir Teddy wags his tail and grins widely, like he's saying, *Aren't I a clever dog?*

I drop to my knees and hug him. My face is buried in his coat so he can't see my sad-happy face. Only I'm grinning against him because finally something I lost has come back to me safe and sound.

CHAPTER 19

"You know I'll have to tell Mrs. Jarrett everything, don't you?" Mama asks sternly. We're standing in our driveway, watching our neighborhood search party say good-bye to one another and go home. A few of the kids wave to us, and one adult smiles proudly. Jake gives us a thumbs-up and calls, "Later!" before strolling to his friend's house with a little grin.

I can't grin back, though. I hold hands with London and Olivia. Okay, I grip my friends' hands so tightly they both turn around and give me identical frowns. I mouth *sorry* and loosen my grip a little. Now that we've found Sir Teddy, my tiredness is covering me like a blanket.

It's like all the tension of today was keeping me energized, and now I'm like an old can of Coke left open on the counter too long. Flat. Exhausted. Not sure what's next.

I know I should be really happy. And I am. But I can see from Mama's face that this disaster isn't over. She's got a lot to say, and it's not good.

London's mom reaches over and pats Mama on the shoulder. "Let's wait until Mrs. Jarrett gets back," she says quietly. "No need to worry her while she's with her mother."

Mama nods. "You're right," she says, sighing a little bit. "But you girls have just been so irresponsible."

I blink. What is she even talking about?

"Irresponsible?" I demand, my tiredness forgotten for a minute. "How? We took care of someone's pet. We made sure he was happy and safe."

"You lost him," she points out. Her face is pinched.

"That's not our fault," I groan. "Dada Jee left the gate open."

Mama looks ready to fight with me. "Are you blaming your grandfather . . . ?"

"She's right," comes Dada Jee's gruff voice from our front porch. He'd taken Sir Teddy inside to feed him dinner. Now he's back, with Sir Teddy leaning against him like they're old friends.

Mama turns. She's lost some of her pinched look. "What?"

Dada Jee shrugs. "I was the one who left the fence gate open. I should have been more careful. I just . . . wasn't thinking when that pesky squirrel ran roughshod over my precious lemons."

Olivia giggles. "I can imagine."

Mama shakes her head. "No . . ." she begins.

Dada Jee points to us girls with his cane. "These girls did a really good job, considering they've never done this before," he interrupts. "Plus, Imaan was taking care of Amir too, with his sneezing and everything. I'm proud of her."

"Thanks, Dada Jee," I whisper. It's nice to be appreciated.

Dada Jee holds out his arms, and I run to hug him. He may be a grumpy dude, but I know he loves me more than anything. Plus, he's Baba's dad, which means he's special.

His hug is strong and smells like lemons. I take a deep breath. "London and Olivia too, right?" I ask. Even though they left me alone to take care of Sir Teddy, they're still my best friends, and

I want to give them credit for being a part of Must Love Pets.

Dada Jee nods. "Yes, I'm proud of all three of you."

"Me too," London's mom says, giving London a sideways hug. "Although I must say, I'm a bit confused about everything."

Mama gives a little laugh, the kind that means nothing is funny but you're trying to find humor anyway. "Which part?"

"These girls have a business now?" London's mom asks. "Since when? Last I checked they were ten years old."

"Tell me about it," Mama replies. Her smile is less fake now.

There's a cough from the street, and we all turn around. A couple stands in front of us. The man looks like Jake, and the woman has Olivia's blonde hair, only longer. "Mom, Dad!" Olivia cries. Then she swallows. "Sorry, I was just coming home."

Her dad smiles. "No problem, honey. I know you were outside helping find that dog."

Sir Teddy barks like he knows we're talking about him. I leave Dada Jee's hug and drop down on my knees to pet Sir Teddy's head. "Yes, we found you, didn't we?" I croon. I'm so happy he's back safe with me that I don't even care how silly I sound.

London says, "You mean *you* found him."

I look up, uncertain. She doesn't sound mad, but I can't be sure. Everything has been so strange with us lately. "No," I insist. "We all helped."

Olivia nods. "Even Jake!" I can tell from her tone that she's shocked at her brother helping with anything. I grin at her, because it seems like we both find our brothers a little annoying.

Olivia's parents move forward and step onto our

driveway. I watch as they introduce themselves to Mama and the other adults. I zone out totally when they start talking about their jobs.

Boring.

I tug Sir Teddy's collar and stand up. "Come on," I whisper to London and Olivia.

We head to our spot on the sidewalk outside my house, a few steps away. The sky is completely dark by now, and glitters with stars. We huddle together with Sir Teddy in the middle, not really talking, just hanging out.

I sigh happily. This is really nice. I'm so glad to have my friends back. I know I'm grinning, but I can't help it. Finding Sir Teddy was huge because it means Must Love Pets is still open for business, and I still have a shot at getting my own dog someday. Having my friends—new and old—close to me is even huger. It's humongous.

"So," London says, a little nervously. "How's your brother doing?"

Olivia frowns. "Wait, what happened to your brother?"

I realize Olivia didn't witness Amir's sneeze-athon last night. "Mama thinks he's allergic to dogs. He was sneezing and crying last night. And today."

Olivia shakes her head. "That sucks. Does that mean you won't ever be able to get a dog for real?"

My hands feel really cold, even though it's summer. Mama will never let me have a dog as a pet if that's what would happen every day. I picture Amir sneezing like he can't breathe, his face red and splotchy.

"I don't think it's a big deal," I mutter. "He was okay when he got Benadryl." Sir Teddy nuzzles my hands like he's comforting me. I pat his head.

"I'm sure you're right," Olivia says quietly.

We study the road under our feet in silence for a minute. Then London turns to me with a bright smile. "Maybe you could get a hypoallergenic dog," she says.

I look up and frown. "What's that?"

Olivia snaps her fingers. "Yes, I've heard of those! Their coats don't shed as much, and they're easier to breathe around."

"Or a hairless dog!" London giggles.

I can feel my muscles relax. "You know what, you're both right. The possibilities are endless."

Olivia is giggling too now. "You mean hairless!"

All three of us start laughing, and Sir Teddy barks along. Then I hear Mama say, "It's bedtime now, Imaan."

I stand up and wipe my damp hands on my jeans.

When I look up, all the adults are smiling big smiles, even Dada Jee. That last part is really suspicious because he never smiles so big. "What's going on?" I ask, putting my hands on my hips.

The adults all look at one another like they have a secret. Then London's mom says, "Would you girls like to have a sleepover?"

CHAPTER 20

Back at home, I watch Mama pick up some papers from the coffee table. London and Olivia have gone to their houses to get their pajamas and toothbrushes. They're going to be back any minute now. I shift my weight from one leg to the other. Sir Teddy looks at me, head sideways like he's asking a question.

I'm also asking a question in my mind. *A sleepover?* Mama's never allowed it before. She always says there's no need because London and I spend so much time together anyway.

And Dada Jee thinks it's totally scandalous for

a kid to sleep in someone else's house. "Americans do strange things," he grumbles whenever the topic comes up. "Why would anyone sleep in a strange bed in a strange house where anything could happen?"

London's not a stranger, but it's still never been okay before.

"Should I order pizza?" Mama asks.

"Perfect!" I reply in a faint voice. Pizza is the perfect sleepover food because you can eat the leftovers in the middle of the night. No heating required.

At least, that's what happens in movies.

Mama looks at me as she dials Pizza Hut's number on her phone. "You okay? You must be tired after all that wandering around outside. Come sit on the couch for a minute." Then she turns away. "Yes, hello? I'd like to order two large cheese pizzas . . ."

Phew.

I guess it's not a dream. I'm actually having a sleepover with my friends. And a dog. My whole body shivers in a good way. How awesome is this?

I squeal and rush upstairs, Sir Teddy close behind me. I straighten up my room, make sure the bathroom isn't gross, and get extra towels from the linen closet in the hallway. Amir peeks from behind Mama's bedroom door. "What're you doing? Where's Sir Teddy?"

I come close and give him a kiss on his cheek. "You stay away from Sir Teddy, you silly goose," I say.

He goes back inside. "I'm watching cartoons in here," he tells me importantly before slamming the door in my face.

"Great idea!" I shout at the door. Watching on Mama's laptop, snuggled in her bed, is definitely a treat. And it'll keep the poor kiddo away from Sir Teddy.

In another five minutes, London and Olivia show

up, and my house is suddenly full of giggles and noise. And barks. We watch a movie in the living room, eat pizza, and drink lemonade. We take dozens of selfies on Olivia's camera, giggling at how glamorous we look on the LCD screen. Dada Jee dozes in his armchair but doesn't tell us to be quiet even once. At some point Olivia decides to paint everyone's nails blue, so we do that. Except Sir Teddy. I refuse to allow the nail polish near his neatly clipped claws.

It's eleven o'clock when we trudge upstairs to my room, clutching our blankets. "Try to keep it down, eh, girls?" Dada Jee tells us gruffly as we leave.

"We're going to stay up all night," I declare.

London yawns and ruins my mood. "I'll probably be asleep in five minutes," she whispers.

Olivia giggles and stumbles on the stairs. "Make that two minutes."

They've both brought sleeping bags. We spread

them out on the floor next to my bed, and I bring my blankets over to sleep in the middle of them. There's no way I'm sleeping on my bed while they're down here. Sir Teddy's close by, and I can hear his snores.

"Shush, dog!" London commands sleepily.

Sir Teddy farts in his sleep.

We laugh a little, then settle down. I sigh. "This is perfection," I say, smiling in the dark. My mood is so different from the night before, when it was just me and Sir Teddy, missing the rest of Must Love Pets. Missing Baba. Tonight, though, I look at my Happy Meal toys arranged on my dresser and only feel happy. "Perfection," I repeat drowsily.

"Agreed!" says Olivia.

I'm almost asleep when London suddenly says, "Hey, what do you think Mrs. Jarrett will say about everything tomorrow?"

I kick her leg. "No bad thoughts on the perfect sleepover!"

I can feel her shoulder as she shrugs. "I'm just wondering."

The next morning, we find out. Mrs. Jarrett arrives back home just after breakfast, her car horn blaring to let us know she's here. Mama's already warned us, so the three of us have packed all of Sir Teddy's belongings and made sure he got hundreds of hugs and kisses. Even Dada Jee patted his head and said, "Good dog." Amir waved from the top of the stairs and shouted, "Bye, sneeze buddy!" even though that made zero sense.

We go outside to welcome Mrs. Jarrett.

"Oh, my baby!" she gushes, bending slightly to touch Sir Teddy's head. He barks wildly and wags his tail so fast it's a blur. "How have you been?"

"He's been great!" London says brightly. "Thank you for trusting Must Love Pets with your dog."

Mama clears her throat. "Imaan," she says in a low voice.

I square my shoulders. I know what I have to do. "Um, Mrs. Jarrett. We want to tell you that yesterday Sir Teddy got away from us for a few minutes."

Mrs. Jarret looks up, her eyes wide. "Got away? Oh dear, what happened?"

I can feel my throat closing up. Ugh, I'm going to be so mad at myself if I start crying. "Well, my grandfather left our fence gate open by accident, and my brother was sneezing, and nobody was looking, so Teddy ran outside. But don't worry, the whole neighborhood got together and searched for him, and we found him in the park with his friend Flash, and now he's here all safe and sound!"

I take a deep, trembling breath. Everyone is looking at me, even Sir Teddy.

"Flash?" Mrs. Jarrett asks slowly.

Olivia jumps in. "He's a squirrel with a white streak on his head."

Mrs. Jarrett smiles. "Oh yes, of course. Teddy's best friend. Isn't he cute? And Flash is the perfect name for him. My grandson watches that show all the time."

There's a little silence as we all wait for Mrs. Jarrett to say something about the rest of my story. I'm not sure what I'm expecting. I guess she'll get mad and tell us we're bad pet sitters. Or cry in worry about her poor baby being lost and scared. But she just keeps smiling, first at us, and then at her dog, like she's really happy to be home.

"My mother's doing much better," she finally says.

"That's wonderful to hear," Mama replies.

I swallow. Isn't she going to say anything about Sir Teddy getting lost? Did she even hear me? London grabs my hand from one side, and Olivia from the other.

We wait a few more seconds in silence. Should I repeat the whole story? Maybe Mrs. Jarrett didn't understand it the first time. I'd been talking really fast.

Mama obviously thinks the same thing because she says, "Imaan was explaining that Sir Teddy ran away for a little while yesterday . . ."

Mrs. Jarrett's smile gets bigger. She reaches down again to pet Sir Teddy. "You were up to your tricks again, eh, my gallant knight?"

"Tricks?" squeaks Olivia.

"Oh yes, he's quite the escape artist. He can find any little space and wiggle through. You have to keep an eye on this one."

My shoulders deflate. "We didn't know. We

were so worried," I whisper. "We searched the entire neighborhood. Everyone helped. All the neighbors with their flashlights and phones . . ."

Mrs. Jarrett straightens up, her smile fading. "Oh dears, I'm so sorry I didn't warn you." She leans forward and pulls me into a hug. "I was thinking about my mother and left in such a rush, I didn't tell you about it. I should have!" Her face is crumpled now, as if this is all her fault.

Funny, because all weekend long I've been thinking it's my fault.

I pat her back slowly. "It's okay," I tell her. "I don't think anyone's to blame, really. It just happened, and we figured it out, the three of us together."

She looks at me gratefully, then at London and Olivia. "You girls have been the best pet sitters ever. So smart and helpful. I'm very happy with your services!"

London grins. Olivia claps her hands. I take a deep breath and let it go with a whoosh. "Thanks, Mrs. Jarrett," I say.

"In fact," Mrs. Jarrett continues, "I was talking to a friend on the phone this morning, and she told me her son Carl may need some help soon. He fosters kittens, you know. I'll give him your flyer."

"Oh Lord," I hear Mama mutter. I grin at her, then turn and hug my friends. "That sounds fantastic!" I tell Mrs. Jarrett. Maybe Must Love Pets has a future after all.

The three of us do a little dance together on the driveway. Then Sir Teddy starts barking madly again.

"Can we take him for a walk one last time?" I beg Mrs. Jarrett.

"Of course," she replies with a smile.

And off we go down the street, the four of us.

MUST LOVE PETS

Turn the page for a special sneak peek of

book #2: *Kitten Chaos*!

MUST LOVE PETS

We're eating lunch when the phone rings. Not Mama's cell phone, but the landline in the hallway that nobody ever uses.

We all freeze and look at one another. "Just ignore it," Dada Jee growls. "Nobody interesting calls on that phone."

London stands up. "That's our business line," she says.

I grit my teeth. It's not like Must Love Pets isn't a secret, but Mama and Dada Jee both get identical annoyed looks whenever we mention it, so I try not to.

"Business line?" Mama echoes faintly.

"We gave that number to a few people," I reply vaguely, thinking of all the flyers we'd made last week.

"Then you better answer the phone before we all lose our hearing," Dada Jee grumbles, going back to his pasta. He's put red pepper flakes on it, and lots of garlic powder. Yuck.

Olivia kicks me on the shin. I move so fast, my chair almost falls over. I jump over a bucket of lemons and charge to the phone, turning slightly as I pick up the receiver. London and Olivia crowd right behind me, eyes wide open. Mama and Dada Jee peek from the doorway. Amir is the only one still sitting at the kitchen table, eating his pasta.

"H-hello?" I whisper. I'm ninety nine percent sure it's someone selling car insurance. Or maybe a wrong number. I tell myself not to get my hopes up.

London elbows me. "Louder," she whispers. "Customer service, remember?"

I clear my throat and stand up straighter. "Hello?" I say brightly. "This is Must Love Pets. How can I help you?"

Over the phone, I hear a loud crash, following by meowing. Then a man's voice in my ear growls, "Come down from there!"